THE
CLOUD HORSE CHRONICLES

Tiggy Thistle
and the Lost
Guardians

OTHER BOOKS FROM CHRIS RIDDELL

100 Hugs

Chris Riddell's Doodle a Day

The Hunting of the Snark

Ottoline and the Yellow Cat

Ottoline Goes to School

Ottoline at Sea

Ottoline and the Purple Fox

Goth Girl and the Ghost of a Mouse

Goth Girl and the Fete Worse Than Death

Goth Girl and the Wuthering Fright

Goth Girl and the Sinister Symphony

CHRIS RIDDELL

THE
CLOUD HORSE CHRONICLES

Tiggy Thistle
and the Lost
Guardians

MACMILLAN CHILDREN'S BOOKS

Published 2022 by Macmillan Children's Books
an imprint of Pan Macmillan
The Smithson, 6 Briset Street, London EC1M 5NR
EU representative: Macmillan Publishers Ireland Ltd, 1st Floor,
The Liffey Trust Centre, 117–126 Sheriff Street Upper
Dublin 1, D01 YC43
Associated companies throughout the world
www.panmacmillan.com

ISBN 978-1-5290-0936-1

1 3 5 7 9 8 6 4 2

A CIP catalogue record for this book is available from the British Library.

Printed and bound in Great Britain by Bell and Bain Ltd, Glasgow

MIX
Paper | Supporting
responsible forestry
FSC
www.fsc.org
FSC® C116313

For Katy

THE MIGHTY WIZARD
THRYNNE

THRYNNE IS MINE

I was once a lowly apprentice, but no longer. I am all powerful now, greater even than the mighty wizard Thrynne himself. The land that bears his name is in my icy grip and I have apprentices of my own. They are weak and deceitful, but that is how I like my apprentices. They know their place and do my bidding, as far as they are able. I have an army of snow monsters at my command and the cities of the kingdom, together with their unruly inhabitants, have been frozen into obedience. The tree wizard sleeps and the three lost guardians can never return – I have seen to that.

Only one could threaten my hold on the land of Thrynne. One special child. I shall use her to make me even more powerful instead. I know her name and my snow monsters seek her. And when they find her nothing will stand in my way.

1

Snow was falling, as it did almost every day in the land of Thrynne.

Winter had arrived when Tiggy was a baby and had never left. Now she was almost ten and had never experienced any of the other seasons. She had never seen the green shoots pushing up through the last of the melting snow in spring, the buzz of bumblebees in the flower meadows of summer, the leaves of autumn turning a russet brown and falling from the trees. Tiggy only knew of these things from the stories her guardian, Ernestine the ice badger, had told her.

Tiggy's world was cold and white, with the crackle of frost on window panes and the whistle of icy winds through the bare branches of the riverside trees. The North River that had once flowed through

the city of Troutwine was frozen solid, and had
been for as long as Tiggy could remember. The
twin peaks of the once-great city were now two
gigantic icicles pointing up at a grey sky. The
snow-clogged houses and the streets below had
been all but deserted – after three years of winter,
the Grand Duchess of Troutwine and the townsfolk
had gathered up their belongings and taken up
the offer of the sand merchants, who had guided

them across the Sea of Sand to the north in search
of warmer lands. Tiggy's earliest memory was
of standing on the Troutwine Bridge holding
Ernestine's paw, and watching everyone leave.
She remembered the merchants' great wooden
machines, the sandwalkers, striding out across
the Sea of Sand, sails billowing as they pulled
long lines of sledges packed with people and their
belongings.

'Why can't we go with them?' Tiggy had asked the ice badger.

'Because, Miss Antigone Thistlethwaite, it's not time yet,' Ernestine had said, using Tiggy's full name and saying it loudly, as she always did when they were in public, as if she wanted to make sure that anyone else who might be listening would hear.

'When will it be time?' Tiggy had asked. It was the first of many occasions she would ask the ice badger the very same question, usually when Tiggy was cold and tired, and they were running low on firewood.

Ernestine would always give the same answer, but she would whisper this bit: 'When the cloud horses return or the time is right.'

But when Tiggy asked more questions, like, 'What are cloud horses?' and, 'When will they return?' and, 'How will I know when the time is right?' the ice badger just shook her head and said, 'You'll know.'

At first this had only made Tiggy ask more questions, but as she got older she began to understand that Troutwine in winter wasn't a safe place. Ernestine was protective of Tiggy, always insisting she wore a heavy coat and a hat pulled down low over her face when she went out to find firewood and telling her not to venture too far.

The badger sett was warm and comfortable. It had been built by an old water badger called Bocklin and given to Ernestine along with baby Antigone Thistlethwaite.

'Bocklin was the last of the water badgers,' Ernestine would tell Tiggy as they sat by the stove, a blizzard blowing outside. 'We're all ice badgers now. He told me to keep you safe.'

Tiggy had lost count of the number of times she had asked about her parents and why they had left her with Bocklin. All Ernestine would ever say was that Tiggy would find out one day . . .

'. . . I know, I know,' Tiggy would reply. 'When the cloud horses return or the time is right.'

'My job is to keep you safe, and keeping you safe means not staying out after dark,' Ernestine would say, 'avoiding the cats in boots and never, ever having anything to do with the elves or their magic.'

When the Grand Duchess of Troutwine and the townsfolk had left, the cats had taken over. They carried swords strapped by their sides, and wore wide-brimmed hats and expensive boots, made for them by the elves. The elves lived in the sewers beneath the city and employed the cats

OLD TABBY ELIOT

MARMALADE MACDUFF

to supply them with all their needs.

Between them, the cats and the elves took almost everything for themselves, leaving the few remaining Troutwiners to forage for whatever scraps they overlooked. As for the cats and elves, their relationship wasn't an easy one. There were many quarrels and plenty of mistrust. The elves were secretive and dabbled in magical wares, which, if used carelessly or misunderstood, could lead to trouble. Old Tabby Eliot's dancing shoes took him prancing off towards the grey hills and beyond, and he was never seen again, while Marmalade MacDuff's thinking cap overheated and made his whiskers fall off. These were just two of the magical mishaps of which Ernestine had heard.

'Stay away from the cats in boots,' she repeated. 'They attract trouble, especially after dark.'

Tiggy had to admit the ice badger was right. For the last couple of years, more cats had gone missing, always at night when they did most of their finding and fetching for the elves. A few times, as Tiggy returned home in the gathering gloom of dusk, she had seen strange white shapes moving through the snow-covered streets. One clear, crisp winter morning, she'd seen a snapped sword and large footprints leading away towards the bridge. And, just the other night, she'd heard the screech of a tomcat that stopped suddenly somewhere near the disused Bakery No. 9.

The following day, as the snow was falling, Tiggy stepped out of the badger sett and made her way along the frozen river towards Troutwine. There was an old timber store behind Bakery No. 9 that Tiggy had stumbled upon the evening before. It had been getting dark and she hadn't wanted to disobey Ernestine by staying out too late – but she had made up her mind to return the next morning, early, before the cats could discover it too. She hadn't told Evangeline she was going out – she didn't want the

badger to worry.

As she reached the alley behind the bakery, Tiggy drew back at the sound of raised feline voices. Cats!

'For the last time, what have you done with Colonel Fluffy?'

'I assure you, Whiskers, I've done nothing—'

'It's *Captain* Whiskers to you!' said the first voice.

'He might be small, but we can still cut him down to size,' said a third voice, and Tiggy heard the unmistakeable sound of swords being drawn from scabbards.

Without stopping to think, Tiggy scooped up handfuls

of snow and patted them into snowballs. She stepped into the alley, took aim and threw the snowballs with all her might. The first snowball hit a short, plump, grey-furred cat full in the face. The second shattered as it slammed into the ear of a taller black-and-white cat. The third cat, long-haired with extravagant whiskers, dropped the sword he was holding, turned tail and fled. The other two followed.

'How can I ever thank you?' said the small elf, stepping away from the alley wall against which he had been pinned.

14

'Don't mention it,' said Tiggy.

'Allow me to introduce myself: Crumple Stiltskin, at your service.' The elf gave a small bow. He eyed Tiggy thoughtfully. 'And your name is . . .?'

'Miss Antigone Thistlethwaite,' said Tiggy. 'I'm out collecting firewood.'

The elf seemed disappointed when he heard her name, almost as if he were hoping for another.

'And where do you live, Miss Thistlethwaite?' Crumple Stiltskin asked. 'Somewhere close by?'

'Not far,' said Tiggy evasively. She knew she shouldn't be talking to this elf – she shouldn't have intervened at all, in fact, but she couldn't let him be attacked by those cats.

'I thought all the townsfolk left years ago, and yet here you are, Miss Thistlethwaite.' The elf smiled. 'I wonder why.'

'I'm just looking for firewood,' Tiggy repeated.

'Firewood? Oh, I think I can do better than that,' laughed Crumple Stiltskin.

He scampered down the alley to the circular sewer cover, pulled it aside and climbed down. Tiggy waited. When he appeared a few moments later, he was carrying a pair of boots and a scarf in one hand, a rucksack in the other. He held them out to Tiggy.

'For you,' Crumple Stiltskin said. 'Only one careless owner.'

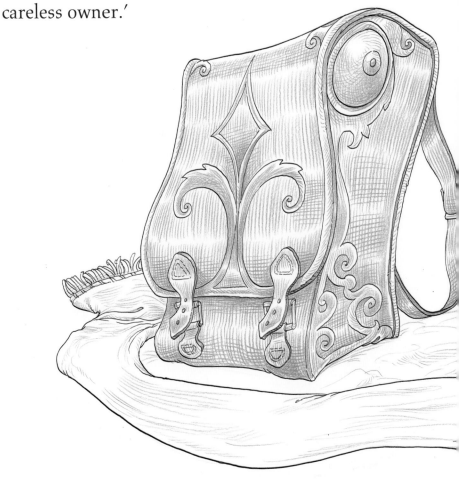

17

2

Tiggy thanked Crumple Stiltskin, who bowed low once more, then disappeared down into the sewer, pulling the cover back into place behind him.

Tiggy stood for a moment to collect her thoughts. She hoped she hadn't given anything away. Ernestine wouldn't be pleased that Tiggy had talked to an elf, let alone accepted gifts from one.

Tiggy looked at the pair of boots. They were beautifully stitched, the soft leather embossed with stars and symbols, the soles studded with tiny hobnails that looked perfect for gripping in the snow. Tiggy's shoes were scuffed and almost worn out, stuffed with strips of material cut from old curtains to plug the holes. She took them off and pulled on the boots. They were as comfortable and well-fitting as she'd hoped they'd be. After all, the elves had a reputation as excellent shoemakers and the cats of Troutwine prized their boots above everything else the elves had to offer.

Tiggy examined the scarf. It was plain, slightly yellow in colour and not nearly as decorative as the boots, but when she put it on a wonderful warm sensation seemed to flow from her neck down. Elves were known for dabbling in magical items and Tiggy knew she should be careful. More than once, Ernestine had warned her about magic and how it could be misused. Reluctantly Tiggy reached up to untie the scarf, when it spoke.

'Oh, please don't take me off,' it said in a soft, silky voice, no louder than a whisper. 'I've waited so long to be owned by someone like you.'

'Like me?' said Tiggy. She felt a little concerned, but the scarf made her feel beautifully warm.

'Someone who has the gift of understanding magical things. I wouldn't talk to just anyone, you know,' the scarf went on. 'Certainly not that fat old cat, Colonel Fluffy, who used to own me. Horribly sharp claws and I'm pretty certain he had fleas too. It's why Boots, Baggage and I decided to run away.' The scarf gave a tinkling little laugh that made Tiggy smile. 'When I say run,' it explained, 'Boots did the running. Baggage and I bumped along behind.'

Boots. The boots Tiggy was wearing clicked their heels together as if agreeing with the scarf. Despite her misgivings, these magical things felt so comfortable. Tiggy reached down and picked up the rucksack. It was as light as a feather.

'That's Baggage. He didn't have time to pack,' chuckled the scarf. 'Anyway, we got as far as this alley when Rumple, Crumple and Trumple popped up from the sewers. Of course, we played dumb, just lay in the snow as if lost or thrown away, but the Stiltskin brothers spotted Boots straight away. "Careless old Fluffy," one of them said, and the next thing I know, Baggage and I are hanging up

on coat hooks in their workshop, and Boots is in a shoe rack next to some dancing shoes that tapped all night long. Horrible smell of glue and a couple of stuck-up harps in the corner. Oh, I'm so glad we were given to you, Miss Antigone Thistlethwaite. If the Stiltskin brothers knew just how magical we are, they would have kept us in that smelly workshop of theirs. No real understanding of magical things, not like you. You understand magic.'

Tiggy felt a pulse of warmth from the scarf. *Why do they think I understand magic?* Tiggy wondered. She wasn't sure if she could trust what the scarf was telling her, but it had such a warm, kind voice. There was no harm in being polite.

'Please, call me Tiggy,' she said. She looked down at the boots and then at the rucksack in her hands. 'So you're magical?' she asked. 'How?'

'Well, I give extremely good advice and keep my owners nice and warm,' said the scarf, 'and Boots are the most sensible and surefooted footwear anyone could wish for. As for Baggage, well, you can see for yourself. I believe you said you were looking for firewood?'

'Yes,' said Tiggy. 'There's a timber store behind Bakery No. 9 just across the alley and it's still got logs in it.'

'Just what Baggage was made for,' said the scarf. 'Let's go and see.'

Tiggy made her way over to the old bakery, pushed open the gate and stepped into the back yard. She crossed the icy cobbles and was pleasantly surprised that the boots didn't slip once. There, against the frost-coated wall, was a stack of twenty or so logs, neatly chopped for the bakery oven.

'I can carry two logs,' said Tiggy. 'How many do you think Baggage can carry – three?'

'Try it and see,' said the scarf in a delighted whisper.

Tiggy undid the straps of the rucksack and placed a log inside. Then she put another in, and another, and another.

'That's probably enough,' she said.

'Don't be so sure,' whispered the scarf.

Tiggy picked up the rucksack. She knew she'd put four logs inside it, but it still felt as light as ever.

'Magic!' she breathed.

'I knew you'd understand,' whispered the scarf. 'Now hurry up and load the rest,' it instructed. 'I'm looking forward to seeing our new home!'

'It's just an old badger sett on the banks of the North River,' Tiggy explained. 'Nothing grand.'

She paused, wondering how to explain these magical gifts to Ernestine.

'As long as it doesn't smell of glue,' laughed the scarf, 'we'll be happy!'

When Tiggy had loaded the rucksack with all twenty logs and lifted it easily onto her shoulders, she set off through the streets of Troutwine. The snow continued to fall. Crossing the bridge and making her way down towards the river, the boots were as surefooted on the slippery sloping lanes

as promised, while the scarf kept her wonderfully
warm and the rucksack was as slim and light as if it
contained nothing but a book and a packed lunch.

Tiggy reached the edge of the frozen river just
in time to see the billowing sails of the ice badger's
snow barge coming towards her. Ernestine was
sitting at the back of the long, sleek wooden craft,
steering it with the long rudder blade. Slung from
the rope, between the mast and the prow, were five
glistening river trout.

Ernestine had spent her day at one of the many fishing holes she'd cut in the river ice, and was bringing home her catch. For a long time, she had traded with the cats for provisions they'd ransacked from the deserted shops and houses of the city – sacks of sugar and flour, jars of pickles and preserves – but over the years, the city had been emptied. Now, the shelves of the larder in the badger sett were becoming empty too.

'Our provisions will last until it's time to go,' Ernestine would reassure Tiggy, 'when the cloud horses return or the time is right.'

Now Tiggy felt a twinge of guilt as the snow barge drew up beside her. Ernestine would not approve of what Tiggy had been doing.

'Jump aboard,' said Ernestine. 'I've had a good day at the fishing holes!' The ice badger was too preoccupied with the river trout to notice Tiggy's new boots or rucksack.

'That's all right,' Tiggy said. 'I'm enjoying the

walk. I'll see you back at the sett.'

'Be back before dark,' said Ernestine, releasing the ice-pick brake and letting out the sails. The snow barge glided off down the North River.

'That's my guardian, Ernestine,' said Tiggy. 'She's always told me to avoid cats and not to have anything to do with elves.'

'I won't tell if you don't,' said the scarf.

3

'So a badger is your guardian,' whispered the scarf as Tiggy walked along the frozen river. 'Where are your parents?'

'I don't know,' said Tiggy, 'Ernestine can only tell me that I was given to her to look after by the last of the water badgers. She was told to call me Antigone Thistlethwaite, to keep me safe, and that I would learn everything when it was time.'

'And when is that?' asked the scarf. The last of the riverside houses was behind them and the badger sett was just ahead, but so well concealed that only Tiggy and Ernestine knew it was there.

'When the cloud horses return,' said Tiggy softly.

'That,' said the scarf, 'sounds *very* magical. And who or what is Ernestine keeping you safe from?'

'I don't know that either,' Tiggy admitted,

'but she has always told me to . . .'

'Yes, yes,' whispered the scarf, 'avoid cats and not have anything to do with elves.'

Tiggy approached the riverbank and stepped behind a large tree root growing from the frozen earth. She reached out and pushed at the tangle of roots. With a creak, they swung aside.

Tiggy stepped into the sett. Ernestine was at the stove with a frying pan in which two river trout were sizzling. She turned and placed the fish on two plates at the table.

The ice badger smiled. 'Just in time for supper.' Suddenly, from behind Tiggy, there was a tremendous crash, and a great white fist of snow broke through the door.

'You must have been followed!' gasped Ernestine, grabbing the frying pan. 'Quick, do as I say. Go to the larder. Behind the last bag of Bakery No. 9 flour, you'll find a box. Take it, leave by the back door and sail the barge upriver. It is time, Tiggy.'

A second white fist smashed through the tangled roots, then the door collapsed inwards.

'Go!' shouted the ice badger. 'Now!'

Tiggy hesitated. All her life, Ernestine had been preparing her for this – but now that it came to it, Tiggy felt awful abandoning her guardian.

'*Go!*' cried the badger.

Tiggy ran to the larder and threw aside the last bag of flour and there, in the corner, was a small, carved wooden box. She bundled it into the rucksack, then glanced back.

In the main room, a huge figure made of snow, with glowing

36

eyes of ice blue, towered over Ernestine. The ice badger swung the hot frying pan, which hissed and steamed as it smashed into the snow monster, cutting it in two. Another huge figure lumbered through the open door and Ernestine swung again.

'Go!' she shouted as the second snow monster crumbled. Tiggy ran up the stairs to the small, round back door and pushed it open. Ernestine was fierce and brave, but how long could she keep the snow monsters at bay?

Crouching down, she ran to the lean-to and climbed into the snow barge. From inside the badger sett, there came a series of crashes. As Tiggy released the ice-pick brake and launched the snow barge down the ramp onto the frozen river, she saw a circle of huge snow monsters advancing on the badger sett.

Tiggy raised the sails and slipped away unnoticed. When she looked back, she saw Ernestine leap through the smashed front door, swinging a flaming broom in a wide arc.

The snow monsters fell back, then gave chase as the ice badger set off downriver towards the icicle peaks of Troutwine. Tiggy blinked away the tears. The ice badger was leading the snow monsters in the opposite direction.

'Good luck, Tiggy Thistle!' Ernestine called as she skated away into the night.

4

The snow barge slid effortlessly across the glassy surface of the frozen river, its white sails illuminated by a full moon. At the ice-blade tiller, Tiggy surveyed the way ahead, carefully avoiding ruts and steering round drifts of snow. Every so often the moon would disappear behind a cloud and an icy wind would pick up, pushing the snow barge suddenly faster. When this happened, Tiggy had to concentrate even harder to make sure she didn't hit a concealed tree root hiding in a snow bank or the frozen ripples of an eddy or whirlpool.

There were no snow monsters following her, Ernestine had seen to that, and nobody knew the North River and the streets and alleyways better than the ice badger. If anyone could give the snow monsters the slip, it was Ernestine.

When the moon came out again, Tiggy could see that she had left Troutwine far behind, and she trimmed the sails and slowed the barge. She was now further upriver than she'd ever been before, and without the ice badger to guide and protect her, it was exciting and frightening all at once.

'What do I do now?' she whispered to herself.

'I would pull over to the riverbank, if I were you,' whispered the scarf, 'and make a nice warm fire. After all, you have a rucksack full of logs, remember?'

It was good advice and Tiggy was grateful to have company, even though that company was a magical scarf who'd run away from a cat, and perhaps couldn't be trusted. And Boots and Baggage.

'Of course you can trust me,' whispered the scarf as if reading Tiggy's thoughts. 'I can't remember where or when I was woven, but I do know that I'm magical for a reason and it wasn't to warm the neck of a fat cat. It's the same for Boots and Baggage. I think we were *meant* to meet for a reason.'

'A reason?' said Tiggy, steering the snow barge towards a clump of frost-covered willows on the riverbank. 'What could that be?'

'I don't know, but what I do know is that when people or creatures try to control magic, use it for their own ends, it nearly always goes wrong.' The scarf wrapped itself round Tiggy's head and warmed her ears. Its soft whispering voice seemed to be in Tiggy's mind. 'I think those snow creatures back there are magic that has gone wrong, and whoever is controlling them is probably responsible for this endless winter. How about we stop here?'

Tiggy pulled on the brake and brought the snow barge to a smooth halt beneath the willows.

'And I think,' whispered the scarf softly as Tiggy took a brazier from the back of the snow barge and set it up on the riverbank, 'that whoever is responsible for the endless winter is the same person your ice badger was protecting you from. She was

protecting you because you're special, Tiggy Thistle. You don't try to control magic – you let magic flow through you as it's meant to.'

'I do?' said Tiggy, and again she felt that mixture of excitement and fear. If she were someone for whom magic flowed, that sounded pretty special. But, also, the snow monsters were after her, which was frightening. 'I'm glad we found each other, but I'm pretty sure Ernestine wasn't expecting things to turn out this way.' She frowned as she lit the fire with a match from a box labelled 'Bakery No. 9 oven lighters'. 'But, then again, Ernestine thought we should wait for the cloud horses to return or until it was the right time – and escaping from snow monsters seems as right a time as any.'

'And perhaps instead of waiting for them,' said the scarf, curling back round Tiggy's neck as the logs caught alight, 'you can go and find the cloud horses yourself.'

Tiggy reached into the rucksack and pulled out the carved wooden box Ernestine had hidden in the larder.

'Maybe this will help me?' she said, holding it up to the firelight. On the sides of the box were pairs of dancing bears and on the lid was a carving of a tree, with lettering beneath it that read: 'Ursine Ballet Troupe of the West'.

'It looks a little like one of the biscuit tins from the old Troutwine bakeries,' said Tiggy. 'Only a little stranger . . .'

She reached out and traced the carved leaves of the tree with a fingertip. The tree glowed, and, with a little click, the lid of the box opened and a cloud of glittering icing sugar rose up from inside and hovered in the air. As Tiggy watched in astonishment, the icing sugar spun in little circles faster and faster until it formed itself into the flickering image of a little princess. The sugar-spun princess stared ahead with unseeing eyes and opened her mouth and intoned in a voice dripping in honey,

'If this lid you can lift,
Then you have a special gift.
To set all people of Thrynne free,
Search beneath the Forever Tree.
Wake the sleeper, true and kind;
Guardians of magic you must find.'

As she spoke, she glowed brighter and brighter and then, with a little sigh, the sugar-spun princess crumbled back into a cloud and blew away on the night air, leaving the delicious smell of caramel behind. The carved tree stopped glowing and the lid snapped shut.

'I said that you were special,' whispered the scarf.

'Yes, but where *is* the Forever Tree?' said Tiggy. 'Who are the guardians of magic? And what's any of this got to do with the cloud horses returning? I've never been anywhere but Troutwine and the world beyond seems so . . .'

'Big and confusing?' suggested the scarf. 'Well,' it continued, 'all I know is that there were three guardians of magic who were gifted, just like you, Tiggy, and they kept Thrynne safe from those who would misuse magic. They rode cloud horses hatched from the magical Forever Tree, but ever since this winter came they have been missing. If you can find them, perhaps they can bring winter to

an end. As for the Forever Tree . . . look at the box,'
said the scarf reassuringly.

'*Ursine Ballet Troupe of the West?*' Tiggy read
the words uncertainly.

The scarf tied itself into a neat bow beneath
Tiggy's chin.

'Go west,' it said.

50

5

Tiggy bedded down in the prow of the barge
beneath an oilskin tarpaulin. The rucksack made a
surprisingly soft pillow, while the boots were snug
and dry and the scarf warmed Tiggy's neck and ears
beautifully. She was pleased to have them with her.

She slept well and woke as a cold, watery sun
broke through the grey clouds, then disappeared
behind them again. Ernestine had stored dry
provisions of oatcakes, jars of honey and smoked
trout in the food trunk of the barge, almost as if she
were expecting that they'd have to leave in a hurry.
Tiggy lit a log in the brazier and boiled a kettle for
tea, which she drank while she ate the oatcakes and
honey. The simple breakfast made her miss the ice
badger.

'I know, Tiggy,' said the scarf sympathetically,

delicately wiping the tears from Tiggy's cheek, 'but you saw Ernestine skating away from those snow monsters. I have a feeling she got away. Think of how proud she'd be to see how well you're getting on. And you heard the sugar sprite's message – you have a job to do.'

'It would be a help if I understood exactly what that job was . . .' said Tiggy, taking a sip of tea. She felt bewildered and a little overwhelmed. 'The sprite told me to *search beneath the Forever Tree* and *wake the sleeper*. How do I find them?'

'If you ask me,' said the scarf, shaking off some oatcake crumbs, 'it has something to do with those bears carved on the box. Perhaps the sleeper is a bear. Bears hibernate in winter, after all.'

'How do you know all these things?' asked Tiggy.

'Oh, I pick them up,' said the scarf. 'I'm a good listener and an even better watcher. The things I could tell you about the bad habits of cats . . .'

'Never mind cats,' said Tiggy, putting snow on

the fire and stowing away the breakfast things. 'You think I have to wake up some sleeping bears underneath this Forever Tree? But where is it?'

'Put the provisions in Baggage for safe keeping,' the scarf advised. 'As for the Forever Tree, I was talking to Boots last night and they were telling me about the Great Wood.'

'The boots can talk?' asked Tiggy, looking down at her feet.

'Heel-clicking and toe-tapping mostly,' chuckled the scarf. 'But I understand them. The father of all boots lives in the Great Wood. And where there's a wood there are trees . . .'

'The Forever Tree?' murmured Tiggy, climbing onto the snow barge.

'It's as good a place to look as any,' said the scarf. 'Let's hurry.'

They set off again on the frozen river as the snow began to fall from a slate-grey sky. It began to get thicker, and a strong gusting wind began to

whip the flakes into swirls, the sails of the snow barge billowing and straining at the mast. Soon the wooden craft was veering from one bank of the river to the other, jumping and crashing back down as its runners hit divots and brittle frozen reed beds. At the rudder blade, Tiggy fought for control while the snow fell thicker and the wind blew stronger. Tiggy shivered, and glanced back, looking for any sign of snow monsters.

Before long, the snow storm turned into a blizzard and, with a sinking heart, Tiggy heard the wood of the mast begin to splinter. With a sickening crack, the mast snapped and the sails went flapping off into the storm. The snow barge spun round, then hit an icicle-encrusted boulder and broke into pieces.

Tiggy was thrown across the ice. The next thing she knew, she was lying head-first in deep snow.

Tiggy lay there for a moment, dazed. Then she heard the soft, reassuring voice of the scarf in her ear. 'Come on, Tiggy,' it whispered. 'Time to get moving.'

Warmth spread throughout her body. The boots kicked out, forcing her up through the snow.

She had been flung into a snowdrift on the far bank. The rucksack must have broken her fall. She scrambled out of the snowdrift into a whiteout of swirling snow and tried to catch her breath. The air was so cold it made her chest hurt, despite the warming efforts of the scarf. She knew she must find shelter.

Just then, Tiggy felt two hands grip her arms and lift her off her feet. *Oh no! They've caught me*, she thought desperately, *the snow monsters have caught me . . .* She shut her eyes against the blizzard,

and the scarf covered her nose and mouth
and whispered in her ears, 'Not caught,
Tiggy, but rescued!'

Tiggy felt herself being carried
through the howling, freezing ice
storm for what felt like some
time. Then, all of a sudden, the
shrieking of the wind stopped.
Her lashes were glued shut
with ice, but it began to melt
and she slowly opened her
eyes. At the same moment,
whoever was carrying Tiggy
put her gently back on her feet.
Looking up, Tiggy saw a tall,
thin man staring down at her.
He had glowing yellow eyes. He
appeared to be made entirely of tin.
'Hello,' the tin man said in a voice
that sounded like rusty saucepans scraping

together. 'It is a very, very long time since I've seen anyone. It is nice to meet you.'

Tiggy swallowed. She had always been taught to mistrust anything magical, and a tin man must surely be magical. On the other hand, so were the scarf and Boots and Baggage, and they had helped her so far.

The tin man held out a large mechanical hand and Tiggy shook it.

'I'm Tiggy Thistle from Troutwine,' said Tiggy, looking around. They were standing in a large underground cavern with a steaming hot spring at its centre, surrounded by luxuriant plants, shrubs and flowers.

'I'm Helperthorpe,' said the tin man. 'It says so on the tin.' The tin man tapped a plate on his chest. Stamped on it were the words 'Helperthorpe Tinworks'. When Tiggy looked closer, she saw that plants and flowers were peeping out from the rivets and holes in Helperthorpe's arms, head and shoulders, unfurling their leaves and spreading their petals.

'You look a little surprised by my appearance,' said Helperthorpe, who was now half flower pot, half tin man. 'Perhaps I should explain. It would be such a pleasure to talk to an actual living person. Since Phoebe Limetree disappeared, I've had no one . . .'

'Please,' said Tiggy, sitting down

on a soft carpet of moss flanked by ferns on one side and daisies on the other. 'I'd love to hear your story.'

THE CLOCKMAKER OF NIGHTINGALE

6

THE TIN MAN'S STORY

I was made in Helperthorpe, one of the five towns that surround the great city of Nightingale, but I don't really remember much from that time. You see, I was clockwork, built by the Clockmaker of Nightingale, the mechanical wizard who ruled the city back then.

My head was full of springs and cogwheels, which tiny mechanical beetles wound each day. The beetles were powered by sawdust made from the magical trees of the Great Wood. I was one of hundreds, maybe thousands of tin men, clanking and whirring, without a thought in our heads apart from following the Clockmaker's orders. And those orders were to march into the Great Wood and chop down the trees.

With our eyes glowing and axes swinging, we

chopped and we chopped. We sharpened our axes, waited to be wound back up again, then chopped some more. Oh, the damage we caused, the destruction, the fear we inspired in the townsfolk. All the Clockmaker cared about were his beloved clocks and his precious wind-up beetles that allowed him to rule over everyone.

Then one day something changed.

I don't exactly know what. One minute I was chopping down trees, the next – nothing. I must have wound down. Then I woke up with a strange buzzing in my head.

I was standing in a clearing in the Great Wood, as still as a statue and turning rusty, with my arms above my head and my hands still gripping the axe.

The buzzing in my head had been caused by wasps that had crawled through my wind-up earhole and made a nest. Later, I learned that the nest was made from an old tree full of magic and, gradually, it brought me back to life. But this time there were no orders from the Clockmaker, no clanking or whirring. There were only soft whispers, like a breeze rustling the forest leaves.

The wasps left as soon as I began to move, and the first thing I did was break the axe in two. Not long afterwards, I heard beautiful music drifting through the trees and I followed it. That's how I came to walk into Clocktower Square with the last of the tin men and a whole crowd of astonished townsfolk following me. And there, sitting playing her magical cello, surrounded by the famous Cat Orchestra of

PHOEBE LIMETREE

Nightingale, was Phoebe Limetree herself.

Phoebe Limetree explained it to me later. She was a guardian of magic, you see. The three guardians of magic had appeared on their cloud horses one day as we worked in the forest, and put a stop to the Clockmaker's misuse of magic. The rest of the tin men had been broken up by the townsfolk. I mean, who could blame them? We had terrified them for so long.

Phoebe, along with the other two guardians, had been protecting the City of Nightingale ever since the downfall of the Clockmaker, and the townsfolk loved and respected her. Phoebe's cello told her that I was full of tree magic, just like *it* was. So Phoebe saved me. She gave me a home in the cottage that had belonged to her parents in Spindle Falls on the banks of the South River.

Those were happy times. I tended the garden, planted trees and grew flowers. Or, rather, flowers grew on me. As you can see, they still do. They give me energy and fill my head with beautiful, calming thoughts. Phoebe's cello and I also became great friends.

But then, one day, Phoebe arrived at the cottage on her cloud horse, which was always a sign of trouble in Thrynne. She took her cello, who had been visiting me, and said they needed to leave straight away.

I remember them flying off as the first of the storm clouds gathered over Spindle Falls. Soon

68

after that, it began to snow and it hasn't stopped for nearly ten years. Nothing was able to grow in my garden, so I saved as many plants as I could and set off to find Phoebe and the other two guardians and their cloud horses. I searched and searched, but there was no sign of them.

In fact, there was little sign of anyone. Winter forced everyone to shelter or to leave for warmer lands. Just as I was beginning to freeze up, and fearing for my seedlings, I took a tumble through a snowdrift and discovered this wonderful cavern. The thermal spring keeps it beautifully warm and my tree magic does the rest. I've been happy here, tending my garden and waiting for winter to end, but after so many years, I had begun to doubt it ever would.

When I found you, half frozen and lost out there in the blizzard, I knew straight away that you were special. So, Tiggy Thistle, that's my story. Now I want to hear yours.

7

Tiggy and the tin man set off the next morning. The blizzard had blown over and now snow was falling, soft and steady, from the slate-grey sky.

'Of course, I'm sorry to leave my cavern garden,' said Helperthorpe as he led the way out onto the frozen North River, 'but I couldn't stay forever, and meeting you, Tiggy, was just the push I needed.'

'I didn't plan to leave Troutwine either,' admitted Tiggy, 'but in the end I had no choice.' She'd told Helperthorpe all about her escape from Troutwine.

'Of course not. Snow monsters with glowing eyes?' said Helperthorpe, pausing to let Tiggy catch up. 'I don't like the sound of them! Seems like someone is misusing magic again. Here, jump on my back. We'll travel faster that way.'

The tin man helped Tiggy onto his back and

they set off once more.

'By the way, do you know where we're going?' he asked.

'Tiggy is gifted,' whispered the scarf. It hadn't spoken all night and Tiggy had wondered if it had fallen asleep. 'She has a feel for magical things. We're in search of the Forever Tree, where Tiggy must wake the sleeper. And then we're going to find the guardians of magic.'

'A talking scarf!' exclaimed Helperthorpe. 'Impressive! You remind me of Phoebe Limetree's cello.'

'Does the Forever Tree mean anything to you?' asked Tiggy hopefully.

The tin man thought for a moment. 'It sounds like it should be somewhere in the Great Wood,' he said at last.

'That's what we thought,' said Tiggy, excited. 'What's that?' She pointed up ahead. On either side of the river, the banks rose up steeply in front of them. A great jumble of boulders, one on top of the other, all crusted in snow and fringed with icicles, blocked their way, while the frozen North River turned into a great glittering icefall.

'Those are the Tumbledowns,' said Helperthorpe, striding forward, 'and we will have to climb over them to get to the Great Wood. Hold on tight, Tiggy.'

The tin man began to climb. At first he managed, just, but soon he was slipping and sliding on the icy boulders.

'Wait,' said Tiggy. 'Put me down, Helperthorpe. I have an idea.'

The tin man did as she said, and placed Tiggy on a boulder. She took the scarf from her neck and tied one end of it to the rucksack.

'Ah!' said the scarf. 'I see. You're going to let Boots do the work!'

'Hold on to the scarf,' said Tiggy to Helperthorpe, then she clicked the heels of her boots together.

Just as she'd hoped they would, the boots began to climb from boulder to boulder, never slipping or stumbling, and taking Tiggy and the tin man with them.

'Magical boots!' said Helperthorpe, clutching the end of the scarf as he clanked along behind. '*Most* impressive.'

They climbed and climbed. The grey clouds parted and a pale sun broke through, and it seemed to Tiggy that they must be making good progress up the Tumbledowns. Yet they did not reach the peak. It seemed that however high they climbed, there were still more boulders up ahead.

As the clouds closed in once more and snow began to fall more thickly, Tiggy clicked her heels and the boots stopped climbing. She realized that she'd lost sight of the frozen falls, and now an icy fog was beginning to swirl around them. It felt to Tiggy as if this winter weather were trying to stop her at every turn. Perhaps whoever had created the snow monsters was also controlling this freezing fog.

'We'll stop here for a while,' Tiggy decided, stepping down into the sheltering gap between two boulders. Helperthorpe clattered down beside her. A layer of snow covered his head and shoulders, and the flowers that sprouted on him had retreated from view.

'My poor seedlings aren't used to this cold,' he said sadly.

Tiggy opened the rucksack and took out a couple of logs and the brazier, along with some oatcakes and a kettle.

'A magical rucksack! I might have known!' said Helperthorpe as Tiggy got a fire going and melted some snow for tea. The firelight flickered on the tin man's metallic body, and the plants and flowers began to peep out.

'Ooh, that feels good,' he said appreciatively.

'It does feel good,' said Tiggy, warming her hands. The kettle came to a boil and she poured out some

tea. Tiggy looked at the snow-capped boulders that surrounded them and frowned. Not for the first time, she felt uncertain about everything. Did she really have the gift for magic that the scarf thought she had? Would she be able to find the Forever Tree in this terrible wintry weather? And were they getting anywhere or just going round in circles?

'I've got a horrible feeling that we're lost,' she said.

The snow was getting worse above them and, despite the shelter of the boulders, swirls and eddies of freezing wind made the fire smoke and stutter and finally go out, leaving the brazier cold and dark.

'By my shivering whiskers!' said a squeaky voice that echoed through the boulders. 'What are you two doing out here?'

Tiggy turned to see a rat step out of the shadows, his pink nose twitching as he sniffed the air.

'Those don't happen to be oatcakes, do they?' he said as he approached.

'Yes,' said Tiggy. 'Would you like one?'

'That is kind of you,' said the rat, who was wearing a quilted jacket and a hat that seemed to have been fashioned from a flour sack. 'But this isn't the place to enjoy oatcakes. Come, follow me.'

The rat set off through the gaps in the Tumbledowns boulders and, hastily gathering up the brazier and provisions, Tiggy and the tin man followed.

After a series of twists and turns that began to make Tiggy's head spin, the rat came to a stop in front of a boulder. Carved into its surface were letters that said 'Tumbledowns Bakery No. 1'. The rat pushed at the boulder, which slid back.

'After you,' he said politely.

THE OLD PIPER

8
THE RAT'S STORY

Welcome to the Tumbledowns Bakery No. 1.

Sinclair Sinclair's the name, at your service. I've got to say, it is lovely to have visitors. I haven't seen anyone since winter came to the Great Wood nearly ten years ago now.

Originally, I was a town rat, you know, born and raised in the sewers of Troutwine. Of course, this was before your time, girl, but I still remember the day that everything changed for the rats of Troutwine.

I say I remember it, but I couldn't tell you how or what happened, exactly. What I do know is that all of us rats were in the sewers of Troutwine as usual, when suddenly we heard the most wonderful music. We all followed it, at once.

Up out of the sewers we came, noses held high in

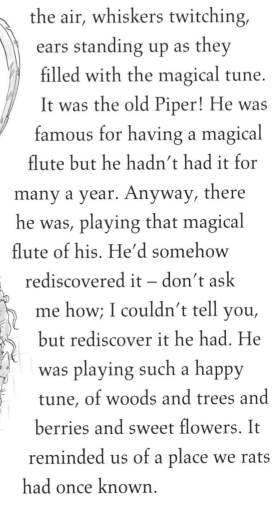

the air, whiskers twitching, ears standing up as they filled with the magical tune. It was the old Piper! He was famous for having a magical flute but he hadn't had it for many a year. Anyway, there he was, playing that magical flute of his. He'd somehow rediscovered it – don't ask me how; I couldn't tell you, but rediscover it he had. He was playing such a happy tune, of woods and trees and berries and sweet flowers. It reminded us of a place we rats had once known.

Then he set off, doing a little dancing jig, with all of us dancing along behind. Out of Troutwine we went, throwing off our trinkets, waistcoats and swag bags. We didn't need them any more, you see, because we had that beautiful magical music and the Piper to play it for us. It reminded all of us, even city- born-and-bred rats like yours truly, of the life rats had once enjoyed in the Great Wood. The Piper was calling us back there with his flute, and we followed joyfully.

Once we reached the Great Wood, the Piper released us from his musical spell and bade us a fond farewell. We thanked him from the bottom of our ratty hearts for bringing us back to nature. It was a happy time, making nests, foraging for fruits of the forest and living the good life.

In spring we cleaned our nests and tidied out our stores, in summer we basked in the glades and meadows, and in autumn we filled our store cupboards and nest cellars down in the tree roots with all the food we had foraged, ready for winter. But then, ten years ago, winter came to

the Great Wood and it never left.

All my neighbours did their best, collecting and sharing food with each other. We rats are generous, you know. After about three years, though, the rats around my tree-root nest began to leave. They were sorry to go, but with their stores gone they had no choice but to set out for warmer lands.

I wished them well, but I didn't want to return to the old city life and, besides, I'd heard the stories of the return of the elves to the sewers of Troutwine and their alliance with the cats in boots. Eventually, though, I had no choice. I set off alone, away from the icy blasts blowing in from the west, and ended up here in the Tumbledowns.

This is where I met Theodora the river sprite. She was the last of the Tumbledowns' bakers, trained by the great Zam Zephyr himself, and she worked in this bakery. She was shutting up shop and returning to the Black Lake until the winter ended, she said, where there were thermal springs. She asked me if

I would care for it until Zam Zephyr and his wife returned.

I agreed to be the caretaker of the Tumbledowns Bakery No. 1 until the winter ended, if it ever does. And I've looked after things here ever since. I've swept the kitchen, polished the ovens, dusted the flavour library and tried to keep my spirits up.

Sometimes I imagine what this place must have been like, in the old days. Theodora told me about how Zam Zephyr created amazing cakes with his team of bakers and his magical runcible spoon, and how he also rode a cloud horse on occasion as a guardian of magic. Ah! I can see by the look on your faces that you've heard of the guardians of magic and their cloud horses. No, I don't know what happened to them. All I can tell you is what Theodora told me, which is this:

Zam and his wife were called away by the cloud horses soon after the winter deepened. He took his runcible spoon with him and was never seen again.

Now Thrynne is still in winter and nobody knows why. I would give my whiskers to discover the reason and do something about it.

Well, I must say, you've got the fire in the oven going beautifully and that oatcake was delicious. What's that you say – you're on a quest? And you want company? Yes, I suppose the bakery could look after itself for a while, now you mention it. But do you really think I could be any help? I'm just a country rat at heart. Yes, I do know my way through the Tumbledowns. The Great Wood, you say? No, I haven't heard of the Forever Tree, but I could certainly guide you to the top of the Tumbledowns and to the edge of the Great Wood. It would be a pleasure. Now, I don't suppose you've got any more oatcakes in that magical rucksack of yours?

9

Tiggy and Helperthorpe spent a cosy night in front of the glowing oven in the large cave kitchen of the Tumbledowns Bakery No. 1. Helperthorpe's flowers unfurled in the warmth, and Tiggy and Sinclair Sinclair reminisced about Troutwine as they sipped tea and ate the last of the oatcakes.

Before they left in the morning, Sinclair Sinclair showed them the flavour library. It was in a smaller cavern at the top of a staircase on the far side of the kitchen. The walls were lined with shelves containing tins and jars and chests of drawers with neatly written labels detailing their contents.

Tiggy picked up a large round jar. 'WARM GOOD-HUMOUR SPICE', she read. Next to it was another – 'RUMBLED HILARITY SALT' it said on the label. There were four little earthenware pots that read 'EARTH', 'WATER', 'FIRE' and 'AIR', and when Tiggy opened the last pot it appeared to be empty.

'What an amazing place,' said Tiggy. On the small table beside a large, comfortable-looking chair was a leatherbound book with 'Recipes' stamped on its cover in gold letters. Next to it was a scrap of paper.

'This is the note that Zam Zephyr left for Theodora,' said Sinclair Sinclair.

'I wonder what this means,' said Tiggy thoughtfully.

'He wrote his recipes on scraps of paper that he pasted into this recipe book,' the rat explained, 'but it doesn't look like a recipe to me.'

'More like a to-do list,' said Tiggy. 'Where is "Other Place"?'

'It is somewhere in the Western Mountains,' said Helperthorpe, trembling. 'It's where the Clockmaker of Nightingale originally came from.'

'The Clockmaker who made you and all those other tin men?' said Tiggy. 'Do you think *he* might be behind all this?'

Helperthorpe shook his head. 'I don't know,' he said. 'I wouldn't put it past him. Someone brought this everlasting winter and someone seems to have made the three guardians of magic disappear. The Clockmaker is as likely a suspect as any – although I don't know what their plan is.'

'This might be useful,' said Tiggy.

She picked the scrap of paper up and slipped it into her pocket.

'I think it's time to be on our way,' whispered the scarf.

Tiggy and Helperthorpe followed Sinclair Sinclair as he scurried through the nooks and crannies between the boulders of the Tumbledowns. The snow was falling as Sinclair Sinclair reached the end of a long, winding passage and climbed up onto a boulder. Tiggy climbed up after him, her boots, sure-footed as ever, doing most of the work. Behind her, Helperthorpe tugged on the scarf as he clambered up to join them.

'The Great Wood,' the rat announced, pointing to the long row of snow-covered trees that fringed the edge of the Tumbledowns.

'Allow me,' said Helperthorpe, picking Sinclair Sinclair up and putting him on his shoulder, then stooping down to let Tiggy climb onto his back.

'Thank goodness for that!' said the scarf, nestling

itself back round Tiggy's neck.

They set off into the Great Wood and were soon surrounded by snow-covered tree trunks with tangles of white-frosted branches reaching up to a grey, forbidding sky. Despite the cold, Tiggy felt a warm, welcoming sensation as they went further into the wood, as if the trees were glad she was here.

Perhaps I really can feel magic, she thought to herself.

'I remember when the Great Wood was all green and dappled with sunlight,' said Sinclair Sinclair, 'instead of this cold, white wilderness.'

From somewhere behind them, a branch snapped, followed by the dull thud of falling snow. Then, to one side of them, another branch snapped, followed, on the other side, by an ominous creaking sound and a crash as a tree toppled over. In front of them, a third branch fell amidst a shower of snow.

'I don't like this,' whispered the scarf. Tiggy peered over Helperthorpe's shoulder as he hesitantly walked on. Suddenly looming up on all three sides were large white shapes, half covered by a swirling frost-laden mist. As they drew closer, Tiggy could see their ice-blue glowing eyes.

'Snow monsters!' she gasped. Tiggy's heart was in her throat. They must have been following her, after all!

Helperthorpe spun round and then ran back the way they'd come, only for their path to be blocked by yet another looming snow monster. A jagged spear of ice whistled past the tin man's head, just missing Sinclair Sinclair, who leapt from his shoulders and grasped a branch of a tree.

'Follow me!' he squeaked.

Helperthorpe cupped his hands together and boosted Tiggy up into the tree after the rat, but before he could follow them a huge snowball hit him in the back and sent him sprawling. The snow monsters closed in on all sides as Tiggy and Sinclair Sinclair looked down from the branches of the tree.

The snow monsters stared up at them, their eyes glowing an even brighter ice blue.

Then they parted and three elves stepped out from behind them. Tiggy recognized Crumple Stiltskin straight away and, from the family resemblance, she guessed the other two must be his brothers, Rumple and Trumple. Ernestine had been right! The elves were not to be trusted. She felt a pang of guilt when she realized she had led the snow monsters to the badger sett, then a hot flush of anger as she looked at the Stiltskin brothers' sneering faces.

CRUMPLE

RUMPLE

TRUMPLE

THE STILTSKIN BROTHERS

Rumple Stiltskin was wearing a hat that was taller than those of his brothers and had more bells hanging from it. He also had an impressive moustache which he twirled as he stepped forward.

'Ah, Miss Antigone Thistlethwaite,' he said. 'You obviously thought using that preposterous name would protect your true identity . . .'

'I'm Tiggy Thistle,' said Tiggy hotly. 'Antigone Thistlethwaite is just for strangers.' She glared at Crumple. 'You sent monsters after me! It was you, wasn't it? After I helped you!'

'She did scare off those cats,' said Crumple shamefacedly.

Rumple sighed. 'Which I suppose is the reason you gave her our boots and bag and scarf.'

Crumple shrugged. 'Elf honour meant I had to give her something in return . . .'

'Yes, yes,' said Rumple. He turned back to Tiggy. 'My brother is a fool, but that's ice under the bridge. You and that ice badger led us a merry dance, but

now we've caught up with you!'

'Where's Ernestine?' shouted Tiggy, feeling her face redden with anger. 'What have your snow monsters done with her?'

'Oh, they're not *our* snow monsters,' said Trumple Stiltskin, 'they just lend us a hand when we need them—'

'Shut up!' said Rumple Stiltskin. 'All this "Tiggy Thistle" needs to know is we've finally caught her and we can claim our reward!'

'Your reward?' said Tiggy. 'Who exactly are you working for?'

'That is none of your concern!' snapped Rumple Stiltskin. He turned to the snow monsters. 'Seize her! And squash the rat!'

As Tiggy and Sinclair Sinclair watched helplessly, two of the snow monsters below them linked arms. Another climbed onto their shoulders and reached out a massive snowy hand to grab them. Tiggy shrank back on the branch, but the giant hand came closer—

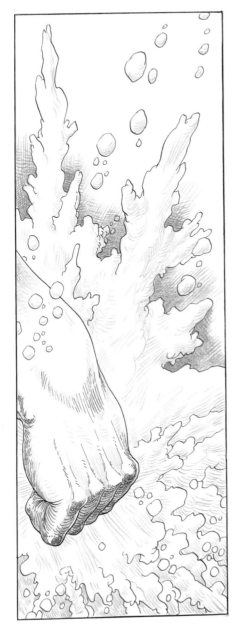

Suddenly there was a blur of movement, followed by a loud *thump*, and the snow monsters exploded into a blinding shower of snow. When the snow cleared, a huge figure rose up with its back to the tree, casting a deep shadow over the three Stiltskin brothers.

Their eyes opened wide with astonishment and their mouths dropped open before, with tiny, petrified squeals of alarm, the elves turned and fled into the surrounding forest.

The figure turned to face Tiggy and Sinclair Sinclair.

'Mote Mulchfoot, so nice to meet you,' it said.

GRIZELL BARKFIRE

10

THE GIANT'S STORY

It wasn't easy being a giant in the old days. The giant-slayers of the town of Beam made it their business to hunt us down. Most of us fled to the Tumbledowns where their carts and crews couldn't follow us, but some stuck to the old ways. The Mulchfoots weren't the running-away sort, and we stayed in the Great Wood, trading fruits of the forest with the goat people of the Western Mountains and their cousins, the upside-downers. We did our very best to avoid those parts of the Great Wood where the Beamish folk lived, and led quiet, contented lives. You see, giants are gentle and shy, despite what the giant-slayers would have had people believe back then.

It was the wonderful Bathsheba Greengrass on her cloud horse, guardian of magic, carrier of the worpal sword, who changed everyone's minds. I couldn't tell you how, exactly, but when I was still only knee-high to a pine tree, the people of Beamish changed their minds about giants, and welcomed us into their town with open arms.

Those were such happy times. We helped out with chores like tree-trunk stacking and tree-house thatching, and they repaired our boots and clothes, and even worked together to make us new ones in great teams of knitters and darners. Why, the whole town turned out one time just to darn Budlee Bristletoe's socks. We brought along the fruits of the forest, great loads of mushrooms, berries and tree cabbage, piled high in the old giant-slayer carts they lent us.

Such parties we had, mending and patching and feasting. Sometimes the guardians of magic would visit on their beautiful white cloud horses, just to check that we were all getting along nicely. My favourite was Bathsheba Greengrass because she

EUPHEMIA RAVENHAIR

was such a good listener and had a special place in her heart for giants who she'd always believed were misunderstood. She married the famous Zam Zephyr of the Tumbledowns Bakery No. 1 – I can see by the look on your faces that you've heard of him. Lovely man and another friend to giants. Grizell Barkfire, the tallest giantess in the Tumbledowns, never had a bad word to say about him.

But then, one day, everything changed. A cold wind blew in from the Western Mountains, followed by grey clouds and then thick snow. Word came from the goat people of trouble brewing, magic being misused as it had been in the old days before the guardians of magic put things right. Foxton Brush, an upside-downer I knew I could trust, told us that the rumour was that a notorious ex-giant-slayer called Euphemia Ravenhair had teamed up with the Clockmaker of Nightingale and they were causing trouble. Creatures were going missing –

the Cat Orchestra and the old Piper. According to Foxton, Euphemia and the Clockmaker were behind it all.

Well, the guardians, Bathsheba and Zam, together with their best friend Phoebe Limetree, rode off on their cloud horses to put things right. That was nearly ten years ago and, as you know, winter has got worse and worse since then and there is no sign of it ever coming to an end.

Now the town of Beam is deserted and most of us have been forced to shelter or to leave for warmer lands. I've stayed put because I am a proud Mulchfoot, but even I was beginning to lose hope. That is why it was so wonderful to find you three.

Now, do tell me more about your quest. Goodness, how interesting. Perhaps I can be of help? The first thing to do, Miss Thistle, is to take a closer look at that carved wooden box the ice badger gave you . . .

116

11

Tiggy put the last of the logs onto the brazier, then reached into the rucksack and took out the carved wooden box Ernestine had given her. Mote Mulchfoot's face lit up at the sight of it.

'Those are the lumberers!' the giant exclaimed, pointing to the carved dancing bears on the sides of the box.

They had spent most of the day travelling through the Great Wood on the shoulders of the giant. They had kept quiet and Mote had stepped surprisingly lightly through the snow for such a large person. They didn't want to attract any more attention from the snow monsters and whoever was controlling them.

They also listened out for the jingle of tiny bells on elf hats, but all they heard was the whistle of the icy west wind through the branches of the trees. Finally, as the snow thickened as it always seemed to do in the evenings, they found a sheltered spot amongst the gnarled roots of a large tree and stopped for the night.

And, as the firelight from the blazing logs flickered, Tiggy, Helperthorpe and Sinclair Sinclair had listened to Mote Mulchfoot's story. Then Tiggy had shown the box to the giant.

'It says "Ursine Ballet Troupe of the West",' said Tiggy, pointing to the letters on the lid of the box.

'I've no idea about that,' said Mote, 'but the lumberers were the bears of the Great Wood who protected the trees from . . .'

The giant hesitated, glancing at the tin man.

'From tin men like me,' said Helperthorpe, shaking his flower-festooned head sadly. He looked up from the fire. 'My memories of that time are simple – chopping and chopping, then getting wound back up and chopping some more. I'm so sorry for

the damage we did to the Great Wood . . .'

'I can see you've changed,' said Mote reassuringly.

'When I opened the lid,' Tiggy said, 'a cloud of icing sugar came out and spun itself into the shape of a little princess.'

'Sounds like something Zam Zephyr would make,' said Sinclair Sinclair, his whiskers quivering.

'She said something like . . .' Tiggy frowned as she tried to remember the spun-sugar princess's exact words.

'*If this lid you can lift,*' said the scarf softly, '*then you have a special gift. To set all people of Thrynne free, search beneath the Forever Tree. Wake the sleeper, true and kind; guardians of magic you must find.*'

Mote Mulchfoot lifted the wooden box up in the palm of his huge hand and examined the carving of a tree on the top of the lid. His eyes widened.

'I know this tree . . .' he breathed.

'Can you take us there?' asked Tiggy.

The giant nodded. 'I can.'

As soon as it was light, Mote put Tiggy, Helperthorpe and Sinclair Sinclair on his shoulders and pulled the hood of his mossy cape up to shield them from the snow. Then he strode off through the Great Wood, taking giant, purposeful strides.

Tiggy enjoyed the gentle rolling motion of riding on the giant's shoulders. With her scarf to keep her warm and the hood above her, it felt safe and snug. But she couldn't help feeling anxious about what might be lying in wait for them. Perhaps, even now, the Clockmaker and his accomplice Euphemia Ravenhair were preparing a trap. If they were powerful enough to control the weather, what could Tiggy possibly do against them? Perhaps the sleeper would know.

On Mote's other shoulder, Helperthorpe stared straight ahead, his eyes glowing a gentle green while, beside him, Sinclair Sinclair kept peering round the hood behind him, his nose quivering and whiskers trembling.

Towards the end of the day, they came to a broad avenue, with shuttered tree houses clustered in branches of the trees on either side.

'This is the town of Beam,' said Mote Mulchfoot. 'It used to be a bustling and happy place, but it is completely deserted now.'

Just then, Tiggy's boots began to tremble, then kick out with their heels, before leaping into the air, taking Tiggy with them.

'What's happening?' exclaimed Tiggy as she landed on her feet in the soft snow.

'Over there!' said the scarf excitedly. 'It's the father of all boots!'

Tiggy's boots – with Tiggy in tow – set off running towards what Tiggy could now see was an enormous boot that had been converted into some kind of house. It was upside down, with the sole of the boot as a roof, windows in its sides and a

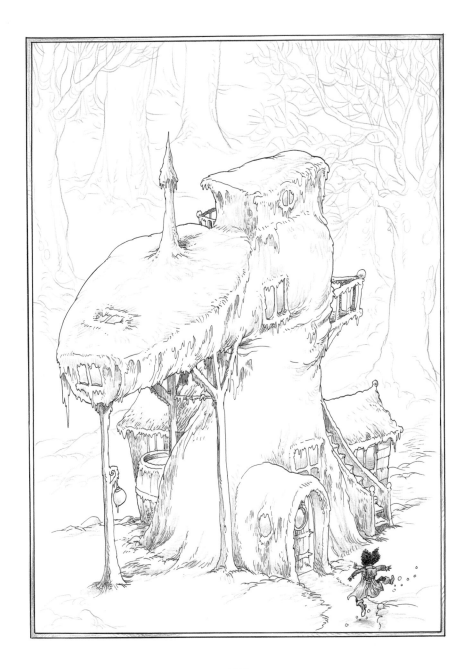

front door, with a sign that read 'The Boot House Orphanage' outside it.

The boot was half buried in a snowdrift, and empty, judging by the shutters over every window. Tiggy's boots did a little jig on the spot as if saluting the giant boot, and Tiggy couldn't help but laugh.

'That boot belonged to Olaf Cloudscraper,' said Mote Mulchfoot, catching up with Tiggy. 'The tallest giant that ever lived. It was said that his boots were made for him by a thousand elves he gave a home to after they fell out with the cats of Troutwine, but nobody knows for sure. Olaf was a victim of the giant-slayers,' Mote added sadly.

'Poor Olaf,' said Tiggy. 'Perhaps he'd be pleased to know that his boot did some good in the end.'

'You sound just like Bathsheba,' said Mote with a smile. 'Now come on,' he said, picking Tiggy up and putting her back on his shoulder. 'We've got to get to this Forever Tree of yours.'

12

They travelled for three days into the depths of the snowy Great Wood. Three days of steady tramping, Tiggy swaying along to the giant's footfalls, and Sinclair Sinclair climbing up onto the top of the giant's head to watch for signs that they were being followed. Each night they sheltered beneath Mote's enormous cloak, which acted as a spacious tent, with the giant's smiling face illuminated by the light of Tiggy's brazier.

Mote Mulchfoot seemed to know every inch of the forest, pausing every so often to uncover delicious mushrooms in the hollows of trees, or plucking snow apples from the frosty branches above. Fallen trees provided ample firewood, Mote scooping them up from the forest floor and splitting the trunks with his bare hands, before hanging

them in bundles from his belt. Sinclair Sinclair had carefully packed Tiggy's rucksack with the remaining stores from the Tumbledowns Bakery No. 1 and Helperthorpe tended the fire each night and helped Tiggy cook.

On the third night, they lit a small fire and huddled around it as Tiggy made some soup with melted snow, mushrooms and pinches of spices from the flavour library: 'warm hope' and 'rumbled hilarity salt'.

'I feel much better,' said Sinclair Sinclair appreciatively. 'I've been looking over my shoulder for snow monsters all day!'

'I feel better too,' said Tiggy taking a sip, 'especially with a giant as a friend.'

Mote Mulchfoot gave a beaming smile and picked up the soup cauldron in mittened hands. 'Do you mind?' he asked politely.

'Not at all,' said Helperthorpe, whose plants and flowers were unfurling in the warmth. The giant emptied the contents of the cauldron in one gulp.

'Got to keep your strength up,' Tiggy said, yawning, 'for whatever lies ahead . . .'

'We can worry about that tomorrow,' whispered the scarf as Tiggy's eyes closed.

On the morning of the fourth day, the snow fell heavily. They had only been walking for a few hours when Mote Mulchfoot came to a halt and pointed.

They were on the edge of a snow-filled dell fringed by ancient trees with trunks so full of gnarls and whorls that they seemed to have grown into faces. At the centre of the clearing, an enormous tree rose up, its bare branches spreading into the sky as if reaching high to catch the clouds. Its huge trunk was frosted white and its roots, twisted and tangled, were banked with snow.

'If I'm not mistaken,' said Mote, 'that is your Forever Tree – the tree on the box. It is certainly one of the biggest trees in the Great Wood and,

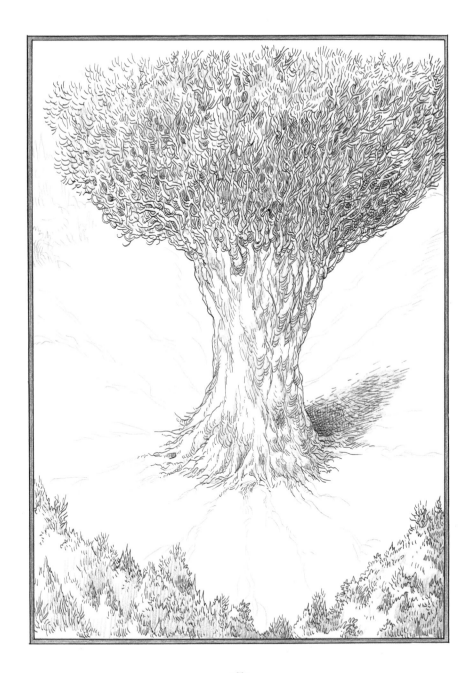

according to the goat people, lumberers used to live here once upon a time, but no one's seen them for years. Lumberers are bears, you know – guardians of the trees.'

Tiggy felt a surge of excitement. The tree was huge, its great branches, covered in snow, spreading out so high above them that she could not see the tops of them. She sensed the burden of winter the Forever Tree seemed to be bearing, and yet, somewhere deep down in its roots, she sensed a small glow of what felt like hope.

'I wonder if it is the tree,' she whispered. 'And, if so, where this sleeper is.'

The giant approached the tree and bent to help Tiggy and Helperthorpe off his shoulders, placing them gently on the ground. Sinclair Sinclair scampered down Mote's arm and scurried over to a drift of snow beneath the great tree, his whiskers quivering.

'There's something buried under here!' he called

over his shoulder as he began to dig. Tiggy and Helperthorpe ran over and started scooping away handfuls of snow as the wheel of a wagon appeared.

'Allow me,' said Mote, reaching down and picking up the whole drift. Gently he shook off great chunks of snow to reveal a covered wagon. He carefully placed the wagon on the ground in front of Tiggy and the others. On the side of it were the words 'Ursine Ballet Troupe of the West'.

'This *must* be the Forever Tree!' said Tiggy excitedly. 'And look, there's a door!'

Sure enough, behind the snowdrift that had buried the wagon was a small door, half hidden by a tangle of tree roots. It reminded Tiggy of the door to her old home on the banks of the North River, which again brought a pang as she thought of Ernestine. With a deep breath, Tiggy approached the door and tried the handle. When she touched it, the whole door seemed to glow and, with a soft click, the handle turned.

'Tree magic,' whispered the scarf. Tiggy stepped inside and the glow grew brighter. She was standing in a workshop full of benches with tools neatly stored beneath them. More tools lined the walls in beautifully crafted racks. The ceiling was festooned with lamps that bathed everything in a rich golden

light. In one corner hung a curtain, and on it was painted dancing bears that resembled the carvings on Tiggy's wooden box. Tiggy crossed the workshop, followed by Helperthorpe and Sinclair Sinclair, and drew back the curtain.

The large chamber beyond was full of sleeping bears. Like a

living carpet of deep brown fur, they were sprawled, shoulder to shoulder, nose to foot, across the floor, with others slumped in hammocks above them or slouched, backs turned, in alcoves set into the walls. Low, growling snores rose from every sleeping bear.

'*Wake the sleeper,*' the sugar-spun princess had said, yet there were dozens and dozens of sleeping bears in front of her.

'Is one of these the sleeper?' asked Tiggy. 'But which one?'

Tiggy lightly shook the shoulder of the nearest bear. 'Wake up,' she said softly, not sure how grumpy a sleepy bear might be. The bear didn't stir.

'Hibernating,' confirmed the scarf quietly.

'Wake up!' shouted Tiggy at the top of her voice, clapping her hands together. Still the bears didn't stir.

'Wakey-wakey!' joined in Helperthorpe, clanging his metal hands against his tin body. 'Time to get up!'

There was no response, just the growling snoring. Sinclair Sinclair scampered over the sleeping bears and seized a furry ear and leaned over it.

'Rise and shine!' he squeaked with all his might.

Tiggy and Helperthorpe joined in, shaking and prodding the sleeping bears, but getting no response.

'It's winter,' said the scarf. 'Bears hibernate in winter and there's nothing we can do about it.'

Tiggy stopped trying to wake the bears and looked around. There was a door on the other side of the chamber with stairs winding up beyond it. Her boots took her nimbly through the sleeping bears and up the stairs. Behind her, she heard Helperthorpe's clanking footsteps following rather more clumsily, and then the *scritch scratch* of Sinclair Sinclair's claws.

At the top of the stairs was a circular room with a bed in the middle of it. Tucked up, head resting against soft pillows, was an old lady in a night cap with her eyes closed.

'The sleeper!' said Tiggy. She crossed the room to the bed and gave the old lady's shoulders a little shake. Just like the bears in the chamber below, she didn't stir.

'She can't be hibernating,' said Tiggy, frustrated. 'She isn't a bear!'

'No. This is powerful magic,' said Helperthorpe, joining Tiggy by the bed.

'We need to think like a guardian. What would Zam Zephyr do?' Sinclair Sinclair added, stroking his chin thoughtfully.

Tiggy looked around. In the corner on a small

stove was a cooking pot, and on a shelf above a sack
marked 'Tumbledowns Bakery No. 1'. As she looked
at it, the sack seemed to sparkle and below it the
stove began to glow.

'I've got an idea,' said Tiggy.

13

THE OLD LADY'S STORY

Oh, my dear little one! You have woken me. And you have been so brave and clever to come all this way and find me here in the Forever Tree, but I fear it might already be too late.

I know it must be hard to imagine, as I am so old and tired, but I was once as young as you. Thrynne was a very different land back then, full of wonders and enchantments. Magic was everywhere, flowing from the cloud palace of the Western Mountains and out into the Great Wood through the North and South Rivers. I was the youngest of the cloud wizards, eager to learn and with a gift I wanted to use for good.

Tree magic was what I studied, with the great wizard Thrynne himself, who gave his name to this land. His daughters, Nightingale and Troutwine, were not as talented as their father, but could weave enchantments that beguiled many and brought them great numbers of followers. But they were quarrelsome and did not respect the tree magic that Thrynne had used to bring peace and harmony to the many inhabitants of this magical land.

I remember, as a young apprentice, how Nightingale and Troutwine broke their father's heart when they left the cloud palace to form their own cities. No good could come of it. Over the years that followed, the cities they named after themselves quarrelled as tirelessly as the wizards who'd founded them. Finally, the two sisters led their followers into a great battle of magic in the middle of the Great Wood. That battle caused the Great Wood to collapse into the rubble known as the Tumbledowns.

Thrynne knew he had to stop any further catastrophe so he created the cloud horses and I, as his apprentice, helped him. The wizard sisters were captured and brought back to the cloud palace where

THE WIZARD NIGHTINGALE

THE WIZARD TROUTWINE

143

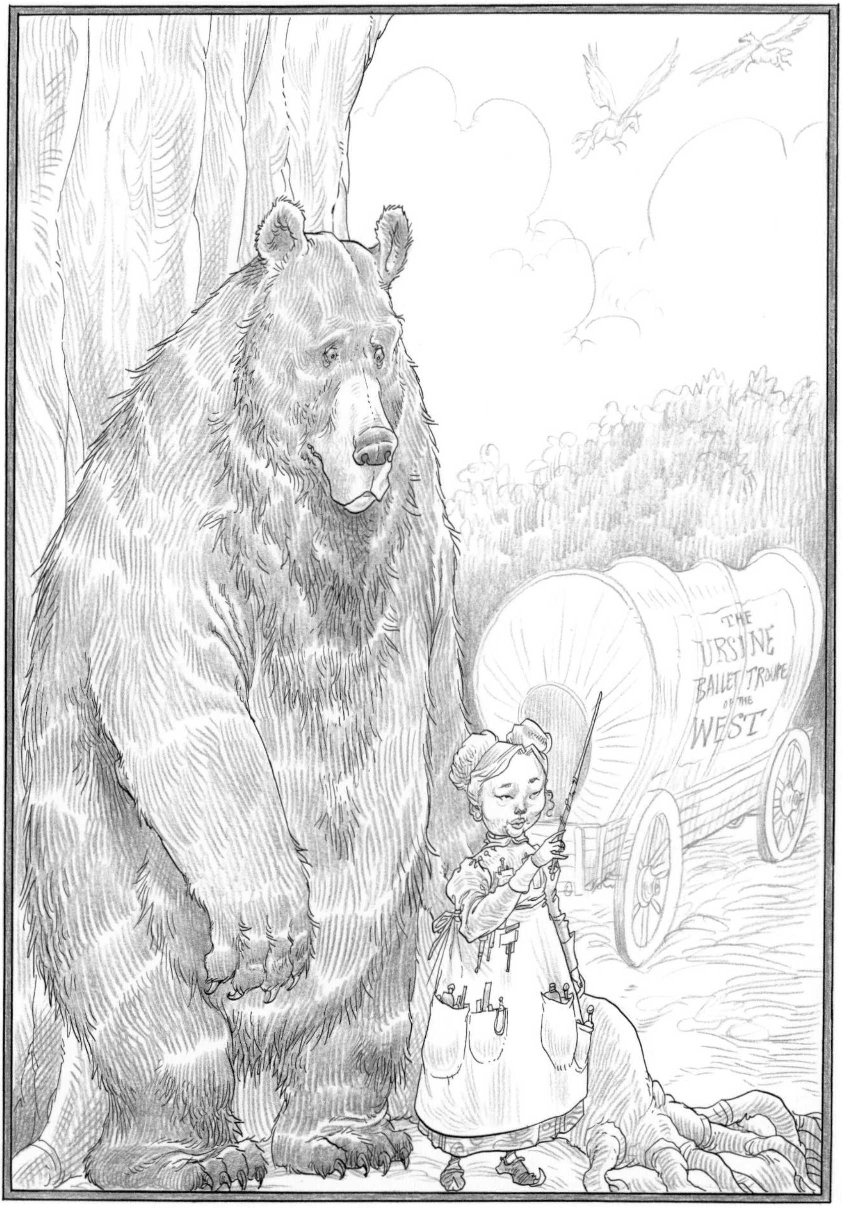
THE
URSINE
BALLET TROUPE
OF THE
WEST

they ended their days, but not before the great Thrynne died of a broken heart.

I left the cloud palace soon after with the cloud horses, and found a home with the bears of the Great Wood. I wish I could say we all lived happily ever after, but, as you must know, little one, the land of Thrynne isn't like that. One day, the cloud horses left the Forever Tree, perhaps because they sensed the world was changing, and of course they were right. The cities of Nightingale and Troutwine grew ever bigger, and then the town of Beam was founded, and magic began once again to be misused.

I did what I could in my workshop, sending out gifts of tree magic, and the bears of this forest, the lumberers, protected the trees of this Great Wood. But that is another story, and for others to tell. All you need to know is that, one day, the cloud horses did return to the Forever Tree and the misuse of magic was stopped by the brave guardians of magic. I was a guardian of sorts myself, in my time, and three more were chosen, magical people who were also fearless and true of heart.

For a time, all did seem well in the land of Thrynne. Then a cold wind from the Western Mountains began to blow and I knew in my old bones that magic was being misused again. The guardians of magic and the cloud horses tried to stop it – I know that much. But it was too late. As the snow began to fall and winter took hold, my lumberers, who had done so much to look after and protect the trees of the Great Wood, fell asleep and I must have fallen asleep with them, for here I am.

Now I am too weak to do what needs to be done: to break the enchantment that keeps Thrynne in eternal winter. But perhaps you, little one, can take my place. You remind me of the young apprentice I once was, and your talent for tree magic might be even greater than mine.

You must go to the cloud palace in the Western Mountains – I believe the wizards call it 'the Other

Place' now. One of these wizards must be behind the eternal winter. Euphemia Ravenhair and the Clockmaker of Nightingale? Perhaps – but for some reason I suspect there is another hand behind all of this, someone more cunning. You must confront them, whoever they are. But, before you and your brave companions leave, I have one last gift for you . . .

148

14

The old lady had woken as Tiggy placed the bowl in her hands, just as Tiggy had hoped. Tiggy had listened to her story as she fed her spoonfuls of the honey-sweetened porridge, and then tucked her back up in bed. She had drifted off to sleep almost immediately. Tiggy, Helperthorpe and Sinclair Sinclair tiptoed out of the room and went down the stairs to the workshop.

The old lady had told Tiggy where to find her gift. Tiggy slid open a drawer beneath one of the workbenches and reached inside. Her hand closed round a soft velvet case, which she took out. On the lid, in faded gold letters, was the name 'Parthenope'.

'Parth-en-o-pea,' the scarf whispered. Tiggy felt a little shiver run through her at the sound of the name

and her fingertips tingled where they touched the velvet.

Outside the Forever Tree, in the cold, grey light, Mote Mulchfoot was waiting for them.

'Did you wake the sleeper like the wooden box told you to?' the giant asked.

'Yes,' said Tiggy. 'Her name is Parthenope and she told us what we have to do.'

'And what is that?' asked Mote.

'We have to go to the Western Mountains . . .' said Helperthorpe.

'And confront the wizards of the Other Place, who the old lady believes are causing this never-ending winter,' said Sinclair Sinclair.

'And how exactly are we going to do that?' asked Mote, helping them up onto his shoulders.

'I'm not exactly sure,' said Tiggy hesitantly as she settled back beneath the giant's sheltering hood. She thought for a moment and a memory flickered. 'Mote, you mentioned the goat people. They were the ones who told you about the lumberers. Do you think they would be able to help us now?'

Mote clapped his enormous hands. 'Of course! Nobody knows the Western Mountains better than the goat people. Come.'

The journey into the Western Mountains wasn't easy, even riding on the shoulders of a giant like Mote. It seemed that the further into the pine forests of the western slopes they got, the colder it became. The winds howled through the snow-laden trees, the snowdrifts got deeper and, most days, blizzards blew down from the mountain tops. Each night, they sheltered beneath Mote's cloak, warming themselves around the brazier, and each morning they awoke to find the snowdrifts were even higher than before. It was as if the wizards of the Other Place sensed that they were coming and wanted to make things as difficult for them as they could.

As they journeyed on, Tiggy's thoughts were full of the unknown challenge ahead. Parthenope's parting words to her rang in her head.

'Trust in your magical instincts, little one, they will guide you when you get close to where the magic is strongest,' the old lady had told her, between spoonfuls of porridge. 'Only then, when the time is right, must you use the gift I've given you . . .'

Tiggy hoped she was up to the task. But first they had to find the Other Place. The giant swayed and tottered as the slopes steepened and the trees thinned and their supplies ran low. Food became impossible to find. By the time they got into the Western Mountains, Mote Mulchfoot was exhausted.

Finally, one morning, they woke up to find themselves trapped in the frozen folds of Mote's cape. The giant was not moving.

'Mote!' cried Tiggy. 'Are you asleep?' Her heart was in her throat. She was desperately worried for the giant.

Just then, a voice sounded from up above.

155

'Mote? Is that you?' it said. 'What are you doing so high in the mountains?'

Above them, the giant gave a weak groan. 'Hold on, big man,' said the voice. 'I'll get the flock and we'll have you back in the fold in no time.'

A little while later there was the sound of digging and voices yodelling through the cold mountain air. Then, as the snow around the giant was cleared, he finally managed to sit up and pull back his cloak. Tiggy and the others staggered out into the daylight

to find themselves surrounded by large, shaggy-haired people with curling horns on their heads and hooves for feet.

The goat people!

'Langdale Triplehorn,' said one of them, leaning on his snow shovel. 'Pleased to meet you. I'm the leader of these folk. Any friend of Mote Mulchfoot is a friend of ours. Now, come back to our fold and we'll get you warmed up.'

'Langdale Triplehorn!' exclaimed Sinclair Sinclair, jumping forward and clasping the goat man by the hand. 'Weren't you Zam Zephyr's chief baker at the Tumbledowns Bakery No. 1?'

'I was indeed,' said Langdale, then he shook his head sadly, his magnificent horns glinting in the morning light. 'But that was a long, long time ago.'

15

Langdale Triplehorn led them along a rocky path that had been kept clear of snow. It followed the ridgeline of one of the smaller mountains, the great snowy peaks of the highest of the Western Mountains towering over them. They came to a series of rough steps cut into the rock and descended into a steep valley. At the bottom of the valley was a stockade constructed of tall pine logs. Langdale stopped in front of the gates in the middle of the wooden wall and, throwing back his shaggy head, gave a loud yodelling call.

The goat people were astonishing, Tiggy thought, as the gates slowly opened and Langdale led the goat men and women, shovels over their shoulders, inside. Unlike the quarrelsome cats in boots and the secretive elves with their magical wares, the goat people seemed gentle and good humoured. Their happy, open faces showed their emotions in much the same way that Mote Mulchfoot's did. They had cheerfully set about the task of rescuing their friend and his companions, all working together, and now they were welcoming them to their home.

Tiggy felt a a tingling sensation starting somewhere deep inside and flowing to her fingertips, and knew she could count on Langdale and his people to help. Tiggy, Helperthorpe and Sinclair Sinclair followed Mote Mulchfoot through the gates, which shut firmly behind them. Mote was instantly surrounded by excited kids, clip-clopping in little circles and leaping up into his arms. Mote was delighted to see them, but Tiggy could see he was exhausted.

'Welcome to the fold,' said Langdale. 'Warm yourselves by the hearth and I'll get you some soup.'

The sides of the canyon around them were

crowded with small thatched pinewood huts, while in the middle was a huge firepit. It was ringed by tiers of seats cut into rock on which rows of goat people were sitting warming themselves and gazing into the fire blazing below. Tiggy saw that on one side of the fire was an enormous bread oven, and on top of it a huge cauldron of soup was bubbling. She watched as kids and goat people in aprons trotted back and forth from the oven to the rows of seats, handing out bowls of delicious-looking soup and slices of fresh bread. The goat people in the front row had long forks with bread on the end of them, which they held out to toast in front of the fire.

As they approached, the flock parted, making room for them to sit down. Mote was given the front row, closest to the fire, and six goat women carried an enormous bowl of steaming soup to him, followed by two more with a spoon carved from a single pine tree. They presented the giant with the dish and the spoon, which both said 'Welcome!' in musical voices as he took them. The goat women stepped back in surprise and exchanged looks of astonishment as Mote began slurping his soup.

'Well, well,' Tiggy heard them say. 'We've never heard them speak before.'

'Tree magic!' whispered the scarf approvingly.

Tiggy was handed her own bowl of soup and wooden spoon and took a sip. She tasted rich beans and barley. Instantly she felt her strength begin to return.

'This soup is pretty magical too,' she said.

'This bread is the best I've ever tasted,' said Sinclair Sinclair, nibbling hungrily at a slice almost as big as himself.

'And the heat of this fire is doing wonders for my seedlings,' said Helperthorpe, beginning to bloom. Around them, the goat people chatted excitedly and were joined from the huts around the canyon by more and more until the tiered seats were full of wagging, tousled-haired and curly-horned heads. Tiggy had had no idea there were so many of these wonderful goat people in the Western Mountains.

'The Other Place!' Tiggy heard the enormous spoon in Mote Mulchfoot's hand exclaim. 'You really don't want to go there . . .'

'We ran away from there once,' added the dish, now empty of soup, 'and we're never going back!'

Mote cast an anxious look down at Tiggy.

'We have to, though,' whispered Tiggy. 'It's the only way to stop this winter.'

Just then, there was a loud clanging sound and, looking across, Tiggy saw that Langdale was banging the side of the cauldron with a soup ladle to get everyone's attention.

'Greetings, new friends,' the goat man said in a loud voice. 'I hope you are feeling warm and rested. Mote, our old friend, it's lovely to welcome you back into the fold. But we must ask – what brings you and your companions to the Western Mountains in the depths of winter?'

Tiggy got to her feet and joined Langdale at the bread oven. She turned to face a sea of expectant faces.

'My name is Tiggy Thistle of Troutwine,' she said, 'and winter is why we've come to the Western Mountains. We suspect one of the wizards of the Other Place are responsible for this never-ending winter and we want to put a stop to it.'

There was a low muttering amongst the flock of goat people, many casting anxious glances up at the grey clouds that swirled overhead.

Langdale turned to Tiggy. 'We've suspected as much for almost ten years now, ever since the great glacier appeared, sealing off the Other Place, and with it came the harshest winter the Western Mountains have ever seen.' He shrugged his broad shoulders. 'We sent for the guardians of magic, who then flew over the great glacier on their cloud horses, but they never returned . . .'

Tiggy saw tears in the goat man's eyes. 'Since then, we goat people have had our hands full defending ourselves from snow monsters with their icicle spears, who attack us for daring to challenge whoever controls them. Whoever these wizards are, they know that we have magic here, and I imagine they don't like that at all.'

'We've seen the snow monsters,' said Tiggy, 'but we still want to get to the Other Place. Can you help us?'

'The only way is on the back of a cloud horse,'

said Langdale Triplehorn sadly. 'Nobody knows of any other path to the Other Place that hasn't been blocked by the great glacier.'

There was a long silence. Tiggy bit her lip. If what Langdale said were true, then their quest had come to an end.

From the front row of seats, there was the sound of two throats being cleared, then two voices said in unison, rather reluctantly, 'We do.'

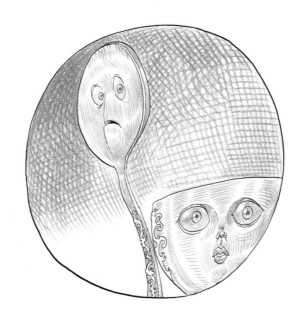

16

'And once you make it into the cloud palace,' said the spoon, 'you'll find the key to the cabinet of magical objects in the clock. The magical objects have been trapped for years and would be so grateful to be set free – and the guardians will want them back. But be careful, because the clock is ticklish.'

'I see,' said Tiggy. 'So we find the ice cave, where there's a tunnel. That tunnel will lead us right under the great glacier, all the way to the Other Place. And then we emerge into the room where you were kept prisoner in the cloud palace.'

The spoon nodded. 'That's right. I dug out that last bit myself.'

'So brave, my love,' said the dish.

'I hope we've been helpful,' said the spoon. 'We've been so happy here in the fold, and what a pleasure

174

to meet a giant again after all these years. It reminds me of the old days on Olaf Cloudscraper's table.'

'Thank you,' said Tiggy. 'You really have been very helpful indeed.'

'Now if you'll excuse us,' said the spoon, 'we need to go and get washed up.'

The dish and the spoon waddled off on their tiny feet towards the bread oven.

'I've never heard them speak before,' said Langdale. 'Not until they were placed in your hands, Mote. Well done, big man!'

'Oh, I didn't really do anything,' said Mote bashfully. 'They just seem to have a soft spot for giants. And Tiggy seems to wake magic up wherever she goes.'

They were all standing at the gates of the fold. Ranks of goat people with long toasting forks were lined up behind Langdale Triplehorn and Helperthorpe, who was wearing Tiggy's rucksack. Next to them, Mote Mulchfoot stood with the great

soup cauldron strapped to his back and Sinclair
Sinclair sitting on his shoulder. At the front stood
Tiggy Thistle.

'Are you ready?' whispered the scarf at her neck.

'I think so,' said Tiggy.

The gates of the fold swung open and Tiggy
clicked the heels of her boots together.

'To the Other Place!' said Langdale as Tiggy
strode out through the gates and up the stone steps.
'Quick march!'

THALIA SLEET

17

Thalia Sleet rose high above the ice table in the central hall of the cloud palace. Ice crystals formed at the hem of her white robe and snaked down in fluted columns, raising her higher.

She looked down at the contoured map of Thrynne carved out of ice on the table's surface. The frozen peaks of Nightingale and the stalagmite towns surrounding it were blanketed in white. The Great Wood rippled with snowdrifts radiating from the great glacier in the Western Mountains, only to avalanche to the Tumbledowns below and the wilds beyond. Troutwine, formed by the two spikes on the frozen North River, rose above the grey hills to the east and the Sea of Sand to the west, now, like the city itself, a white desert.

Thalia Sleet, wizard of winter, sorceress of

snow and empress of ice, had Thrynne in her grip. Nobody had noticed her at first, but then that was hardly surprising. The wizards of the Other Place had always been wrapped up in their own magical ambitions, stretching back to the time of the great wizard Thrynne himself. It had been easy to let them think that she was a nobody, easy to take control of more and more magic until she held them all in her thrall. And it was even easier to trick the guardians of magic into their icy prison.

The Clockmaker and Euphemia Ravenhair – idiots, easily distracted by their own petty desires – bent easily to her will, and all the other wizards were now prisoners and the creatures below kept quiet by the eternal winter and the snow monsters.

The one thing that continued to elude Thalia Sleet was the child. The child was the only one who could stop her. Until she had them, her power would never be secure . . .

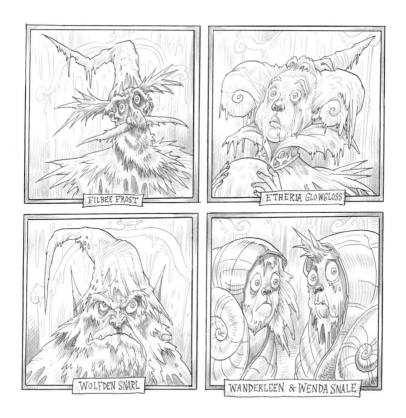

FILBEE FROST

ETHERIA GLOWGLOSS

WOLFDEN SNARL

WANDERLEEN & WENDA SNALE

Thalia cast her icy gaze on the figures fused to
their crystal thrones on either side of the table.
Old Filbee Frost, who'd taught her the rudiments
of weather magic, sat frozen to the spot next to
Etheria Glowgloss, still clutching the remains of her
shattered crystal ball in her jewelled fingers. On the
other side, Wolfden Snarl, his mane of crimson hair

now sticking up in shards like an exploded snowball, stared straight ahead.

Thalia smiled. 'Not such a bully now . . .'

Wanderleen and Wenda Snale, frozen in their shells, sat on either side of the once-powerful wizard, their eyes as glassy as his.

'All of you taught me in your different ways,' Thalia admitted, 'right up until the moment I froze you to the spot.'

'Ten years ago,' said the Clockmaker from the far end of the table. Not for the first time, he was grateful for the dark tint to his spectacles that hid the fear in his eyes. 'Your power is now unparalleled, Your Highness.'

'It is indeed.' Euphemia Ravenhair nodded her head vigorously. 'A little music to celebrate?' She clicked her fingers and in the icicle-fringed balcony above, an orchestra of cats with glazed, unblinking eyes began to play as an old figure in a patchwork suit held a non-existent flute to his lips with one hand and conducted them with the other.

'Keeping up with your enchantment classes, I see,' said Thalia Sleet with a thin smile. She turned back to the Clockmaker. 'Your apprentice is doing well. I wish the same could be said for your cats in boots and those elves. Have they found the girl or not?'

The Clockmaker seemed to shrink into the crystal chair on which he was sitting, but he waved a hand airily in the direction of Troutwine.

'The cats and elves have been quarrelling as usual,' he said, 'but the Stiltskin brothers tracked the girl down in the Great Wood with

the help of our snow guards.'

'And?' said Thalia, shards of ice falling from her gown and shattering across the floor as she descended to the ground.

'That was the last I heard from them,' admitted the Clockmaker. 'But I'm sure they've got everything under control, Your Highness. After all, Parthenope is still fast asleep and Thrynne is still in winter.'

Thalia turned her back on the two of them and crossed the hall to the window. Outside in the huge courtyard, the great ice pyramid stood flanked on all sides by her snow guards. She raised a finger, and a thousand pairs of glowing eyes turned towards hers. The cold slowed down everything, the ice freezing things to a standstill, snow muffling and taming all that swirling magic, so difficult to control. Now, with Thrynne in winter, it was all hers. Soon, the rest of the land would follow.

'If you'll excuse me, Your Highness,' said the

Clockmaker, rising from his crystal chair and backing nervously away, 'I just need to go and wind up my clock.'

He left the room. Thalia watched him go. Then she felt a hand on her sleeve.

'I really think the Clockmaker has lost his touch,' said Euphemia Ravenhair. 'He is stalling because he's afraid that the Stiltskin brothers have failed. Give me control of the snow guards and I'll bring you the girl.'

'What about the Clockmaker?' said Thalia, arching an eyebrow.

Euphemia smiled. 'He can join the other wizards at the ice table.'

From a room a little way off came the sound of a clock chiming, followed by a strangulated cry and a loud crash.

'What was that?' demanded Thalia, rising up on a column of ice and silencing the cat orchestra with a wave of her hand.

'I'll go and see, Your Highness,' said Euphemia, 'but I told you the Clockmaker's losing his touch . . .'

18

Tiggy's boots took her up the tunnel from the ice cave to a hole in the floor of the room containing the cabinet of magical objects. It was where the giant dish and spoon had spent so much time before they'd managed to slip away unnoticed.

They'd been in a drawer at the bottom of the cabinet, far less important than the objects chained up in the glass-fronted display case above. Every night for months, the spoon had pushed open the drawer and slipped behind the clock in the corner to dig through the wooden floor and down through the frozen earth below. Finally, the spoon had broken into the ice cave and had run away with the dish.

Now, Tiggy climbed out of the hole and peered round the side of the clock. She gently opened the case below the clockface, avoiding the swinging

190

pendulum, and her hand closed over a key hanging from the hook inside. The clock trembled as she withdrew her hand and then began to chime furiously. Tiggy trembled too, but that tingling feeling rose from deep within her. She must trust her instincts, she told herself, as the chimes echoed around the room.

A tall man with tinted glasses rushed into the room and gave a loud cry of alarm at the sight of the clock's open case. Tiggy shoved with all her might against the back of the clock, which toppled forward and crashed down on top of the startled figure.

Tiggy dashed over to the cabinet and opened the display case. She unlocked the padlock and unchained the objects inside. A curved fork, a gleaming sword, a flute and a cello case. Hurriedly she thrust them into her rucksack, which absorbed them easily. Tiggy made for the door, only to find her way blocked by a furious-looking woman with deep-black hair.

'Stop, thief!' screamed the woman, only for Tiggy's scarf to unwind and leap at the woman's face. It wound itself tightly into a blindfold as Tiggy felt one of her boots kick forward and take the woman's legs out from under her.

As the woman fell, the scarf shot back to Tiggy's shoulders and the boots began to run down the corridor and out through a huge doorway. Tiggy skidded to a stop on the snowy paving stones of a vast courtyard.

At the far side, Mote Mulchfoot had broken down the gates, and the goat people were streaming through with red-hot toasting forks. Outside, Tiggy could see Helperthorpe stoking the fire in her brazier, which heated the huge cauldron that Mote had filled with snow. At the centre of the courtyard, a great pyramid rose up, its frosted sides guarded by rank after rank of snow monsters.

Tiggy felt the familiar tingling feeling growing stronger. She did not know what this pyramid was, but she knew it was powerful magic. As Tiggy watched, a window in the cloud palace behind her was flung open, and a wizard with white, icicle-tipped hair and long white robes leapt high into the air.

Surely, Tiggy thought, she would hurt herself. But as the wizard approached the ground, feet first, the hem of her robe extended into tendrils of ice that broke her fall as they rooted themselves to the ground. The wizard towered over her

snow monsters, and her eyes met Tiggy's.

'You,' she hissed. Then she pointed towards Mote and the goat people. 'Attack!' she screamed.

The snow monsters' eyes glowed blue as they lowered their icicle spears and advanced.

Tiggy turned and darted into the crowd. She caught flashes of the battle as she ran – Mote Mulchfoot lifted the cauldron of boiling water and at Sinclair Sinclair's tap on his shoulder emptied it across the paving stones. The tide broke against the ranks of the snow monsters in a great cloud of steam. As it cleared, the goat people advanced with their toasting forks, melting the icicle spears thrust at them.

In the melee, Tiggy ran towards the pyramid unnoticed. All around her, the snow battle raged. She reached the pyramid's frosted side. She put the objects down, reached into her pocket and took out the silk case Parthenope had given her. She opened it and took out the beautiful wooden wand inside.

The words she'd heard throughout her childhood came back to her.

When the cloud horses return or the time is right.

Now was the time. Tiggy felt the tree magic surging through her. She stepped forward and touched the side of the pyramid with the glowing wand. Instantly, the frosted sides of the pyramid cleared, and through its glassy surface Tiggy saw a sight that took her breath away.

Within it were three magnificent cloud horses, with wings outstretched and manes flowing, frozen in ice. On them sat the three guardians of magic: Zam Zephyr, Bathsheba Greengrass, Phoebe Limetree. They looked wonderful and magical and . . . familiar somehow.

Heat spiralled out from the tip of Tiggy's wand and the great pyramid of ice turned instantly to water and crashed over the ranks of snow monsters,

197

sweeping them away like slush in the spring. As they did so, the ice pillars melted at the hem of Thalia Sleet's robes, sending her crashing down to the paving stones.

Tiggy felt exhilarated. She had found the lost guardians, and the tree magic seemed to sparkle in the air around them.

The guardians stood blinking in the daylight, their expressions changing from dazed bewilderment to growing joy. Tiggy reached into her rucksack and grasped the runcible spoon, which she handed to Zam Zephyr, the worpal sword, which she gave to Bathsheba Greengrass, and, lastly, the cello case, which Phoebe Limetree enfolded in an embrace.

'I've missed you,' said Phoebe.

And then a voice came from behind Tiggy, a voice that made her blood freeze.

'Not so fast, guardians of magic,' it said icily.

200

19

Thalia Sleet stood before Tiggy and the three guardians, jagged shards of ice springing from her fingers and the hem of her robes refreezing the snowmelt at her feet.

But the guardians were armed now. Zam Zephyr held up the runcible spoon, which glowed with a dazzling white light as his cloud horse beat its wings and rose up to hover in the sky. Bathsheba Greengrass raised her worpal sword, her cloud horse leaping into the air, while Phoebe Limetree took her cello from its case and jumped from her cloud horse to the ground.

As Phoebe's cloud horse rose to hover above her, she drew her bow across the cello's strings. In answer, the music of the cat orchestra flowed into the courtyard from the cloud-palace windows all

around. The skies cleared and the sun shone down from a clear blue sky. Tiggy felt a warm breeze wafted by the cloud horses' wings on her face.

'You stole Parthenope's gifts from us,' said Zam to Thalia.

'Sneaking into my bakery . . . sending those elves to replace my sword with a copy . . .' said Bathsheba.

'And kidnapping my cello . . .' said Phoebe. 'You knew we had no choice but to follow them.'

Thalia shifted uneasily. 'I was only borrowing them,' she said.

Tiggy lifted the wand. 'And you stole Parthenope's wand,' she said loudly.

Thalia's eyes widened and her cheeks blanched. 'It *is* you,' she whispered. 'The child with magic – and you have Parthenope's wand!'

Tiggy lifted her chin. 'That's right,' she said firmly.

'Wait! Wait!' Thalia screeched. 'I apologize! I would have released the guardians . . . one day . . .

Stop! . . . Stop!'

The runcible spoon, the worpal sword, the cello, and the wand in Tiggy's trembling hand glowed brighter and brighter.

In front of them, Thalia Sleet was melting, her white hair wilting, then streaming into water as it ran in rivulets down her dissolving robes, until she shrank into a head and shoulders that stared back at them with wide, startled eyes. With a gurgling shriek, she melted into a puddle, which gently steamed on the paving stones of the courtyard. From all around Tiggy, the courtyard of the cloud palace filled with the cheers of the goat people.

Helperthorpe, his head and shoulders a mass
of blossom, rushed over and embraced Phoebe
Limetree and her cello. They were soon joined by
the cat orchestra, stretching and miaowing and
waving their instruments above their heads. Behind
them came the old Piper, who stood blinking in the
daylight and holding his face up to the warmth of
the sun. Tiggy beckoned to Sinclair Sinclair, who
came scampering over, his whiskers quivering with
joy. She reached into her pocket and handed the rat
the last of the magical objects that she'd taken from
the cabinet.

'Give this back to the Piper,' she said, handing
Sinclair Sinclair the flute.

Just then there was a loud exclamation of
joy as Mote Mulchfoot rushed up to Bathsheba
Greengrass, who leapt from her cloud horse into his
arms.

'Miss Bathsheba!' the giant exclaimed. 'Is winter
really over?'

Zam Zephyr had also got down from his cloud horse and was deep in conversation with Langdale Triplehorn. Langdale waved to Tiggy.

'Come here, child,' he said,

When Tiggy approached, she could see tears in both Zam's and Langdale's eyes. Suddenly two arms enfolded her, and Bathsheba Greengrass pressed her close. She felt Bathsheba's warm tears on her neck.

'She's really missed you,' whispered the scarf.

Tiggy stepped back as Bathsheba let go, and Zam took Bathsheba's hand. Tiggy reached into her pocket and took out the scrap of paper she'd taken from the Tumbledowns Bakery No. 1. She pointed to the last thing on the list.

BOCKLIN THE WATER BADGER

'Am I the baby you asked the water badger to babysit?'

Both Zam and Bathsheba swept her up in their arms as, around them, everyone cheered in the warm sunlight. She knew them, Tiggy thought. She had known them all along.

'You're our little girl,' they said, 'and we're so proud of you.'

20

'Phoebe has taken Helperthorpe back to her cottage in Spindle Falls,' said Bathsheba as she brushed her daughter's hair. 'She said she'll meet us at the Forever Tree.'

They were sitting in Bathsheba's girlhood room in the Boot House Orphanage, which Tiggy and her parents had spring cleaned thoroughly. At last, all Tiggy's questions had been answered. Ernestine had been right. The time had been right, the cloud horses *had* returned and all was well in the land of Thrynne. The long winter was over.

'The Forever Tree?' said Tiggy. 'Does that mean we're going to fly there on your cloud horse?'

The journey from the cloud palace above the Western Mountains and on over the Great Wood to the town of Beam, sitting behind her mother on her cloud horse, had been the most amazing experience of Tiggy's life so far. And Tiggy knew she'd had some amazing experiences since leaving Ernestine's sett in Troutwine.

Thrynne was shaking off winter, and coming back to life. The wizards of the Other Place had thawed out in their seats at the melted ice table, and had promised Zam and the other guardians to be more careful in future. Langdale Triplehorn had assured Zam that he and the goat people would make sure the wizards kept their word. There was no sign of the Clockmaker or his apprentice, but Langdale was sure the goat people would find them. The Stiltskins had apologized profusely and had promised to have nothing to do with bad magic ever again. Tiggy half believed them.

Sinclair Sinclair had gone back to reopen the Tumbledowns Bakery No. 1 with Zam, and the news was that the old bakers were returning. Ernestine had escaped from the snow monsters and hidden

in Troutwine until the thaw and was now a proper water badger. Tiggy couldn't wait to see her again and sail with her on the waters of the North River. Troutwine was filling up once more with people returning from the Sea of Sand, and the cats had been told to give up their boots and mend their ways. The elves, meanwhile, were keeping a low profile down in the sewers, which was probably for the best.

'Your father will be back from the Tumbledowns this evening in time for Mote's party, and then we'll fly to the Forever Tree tomorrow, Tiggy.'

Tiggy liked it when her mother called her Tiggy.

Bathsheba had explained that Miss Antigone Thistlethwaite had been the name old Bocklin the water badger had given her in order to keep her safe from the wizards of the Other Place. All the baby had had was a wooden box, which her mother had tucked in amongst her clothing. He had been looking after Tiggy when news came that the three guardians had visited the Other Place, never to return. Thalia knew Zam and Bathsheba had a daughter named after the wood wizard Parthenope and had searched for her throughout Thrynne. As the last guardian of magic still free, she feared Tiggy would be able to stop their plans. Thalia had been right.

'Parthenope Zephyr-Greengrass,' Tiggy had repeated after her mother, then smiled. 'But Tiggy for short!'

*

That evening, the town of Beam was full of
returners – upside-downers, Beamish folk and
giants – all celebrating the end of winter and the
return of the guardians of magic.

'You're a guardian of magic now, Tiggy,' Mote
Mulchfoot said as they sat by the fire in the town
square. 'Just like your mother and father.'

'I suppose so,' said Tiggy, 'but I can't help feeling
that something's missing . . .'

The next morning, Tiggy climbed up beside her
father, Zam, on his magnificent cloud horse. Zam
stroked the horse's white neck and, leaning forward,
looked into its sky-blue eyes. The cloud horse gave a
snort, and then broke into a trot, then a gallop, as it
began to flap its great feathered wings.

Tiggy felt her stomach dip and flutter as they rose
above the tree houses of Beam and swept off over
the Great Wood. In and out of high, tumbling clouds

they flew, steadily and gracefully, before swooping down as they approached the towering Forever Tree.

They circled the topmost branches, now green with new leaves, Bathsheba and her cloud horse joining them. In the distance, another cloud horse appeared, and Tiggy recognized the figure of Phoebe Limetree, and waved. Looking down, Tiggy saw a nest in the branches below, with fragments of eggshell nestled in its centre.

Zam's cloud horse spread its wings wide and came down to land beside the workshop door in a graceful arc. Bathsheba and Phoebe joined them.

The lumberers were waiting. They were wide awake after their long hibernation and eager to get back to work. Their eyes were glistening, their fur sleek, their noses shiny and their covered wagon newly painted. On its side was a new sign that read: 'The Lumberers: Caretakers of the Great Wood'.

When the head lumberer saw Tiggy looking at the wagon, he smiled and said, 'We don't have to disguise ourselves as dancing bears any more.'

'Just as well,' said a kindly voice. The bears parted as the old lady stepped out of the workshop. Tiggy rushed forward, the velvet case in her hand, only for the old lady to shake her head.

'No, little one, the wand is yours.' She smiled. 'From one Parthenope to another. And I have another gift for you . . .'

She stepped away from the workshop door and a cloud horse foal trotted out and came over to nuzzle Tiggy's hand.

'My own cloud horse!' exclaimed Tiggy as her scarf gave a delighted gasp.

Her parents placed their hands on her shoulders. 'You're a guardian of magic now,' they said.

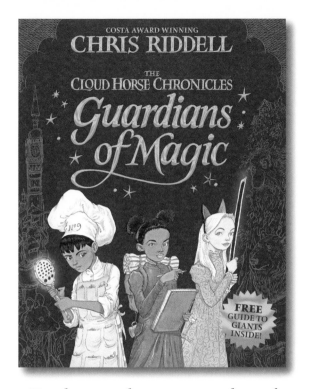

'By the award-winning author of
Tiggy Thistle and the Lost Guardians'

For as long as anyone can remember, children have made
a wish on a cloud horse, never *quite* believing that their
wishes will come true. But times are changing. The future
of magic is in danger. Enemies are working together to
destroy it – especially the magic of nature and its most
powerful source, The Forever Tree. Unless three brave
children fight back and believe in the impossible, soon
magic and the cloud horses will be gone. Zam, Phoebe and
Bathsheba don't yet know how powerful they are . . .

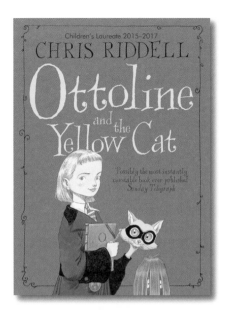

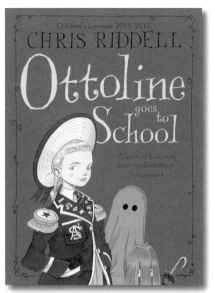

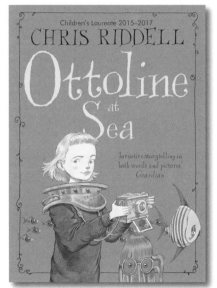

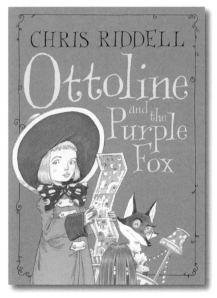

Also by Chris Riddell and available from
Macmillan Children's Books

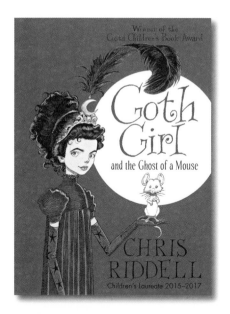

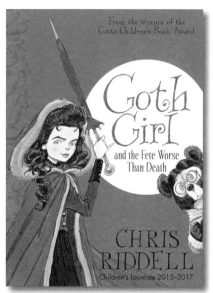

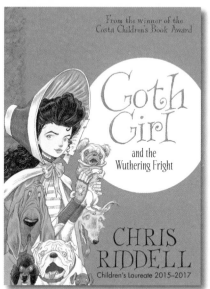

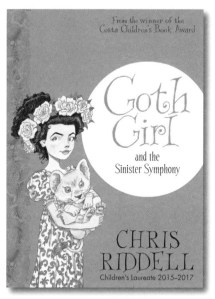

Also by Chris Riddell and available from
Macmillan Children's Books